Ghost Breezes

short stories
Daniel Lillford

*Illustrations by
Jesse Lillford-Brighton*

© 2022 Daniel Lillford

All rights reserved. No part of this book may be reproduced or transmitted in any form or by any means, electronic or mechanical, including photocopying, or by any information storage or retrieval system, without permission in writing from the publisher.

Cover and interior art: Jesse Lillford-Brighton
Cover design: Rebekah Wetmore
Editor: Andrew Wetmore

ISBN: 978-1-990187-42-1
First edition November, 2022

Moose House
Publications

2475 Perotte Road
Annapolis County, NS
B0S 1A0

moosehousepress.com
info@moosehousepress.com

We live and work in Mi'kma'ki, the ancestral and unceded territory of the Mi'kmaw People. This territory is covered by the "Treaties of Peace and Friendship" which Mi'kmaw and Wolastoqiyik (Maliseet) People first signed with the British Crown in 1725. The treaties did not deal with surrender of lands and resources but in fact recognized Mi'kmaq and Wolastoqiyik (Maliseet) title and established the rules for what was to be an ongoing relationship between nations. We are all Treaty people.

Foreword

The stories within are from a timeless landscape. There are few references to place names or concrete time periods, although I imagine this landscape, and this collection, as a tribute to Nova Scotia.

The slightly indeterminate quality of the landscape enables place to act at times as a *relief*, as a background for almost biblical stories of human lives. At other times this landscape also appears forceful, not to be ignored, neither by the characters in the stories, nor us, the readers.

What I mean by 'biblical' is in the sense that these are stories of characters and their life lessons. But these life lessons do not prescribe an obvious sense of morality. They are foundational stories; there is love, infidelity, sentimentality and loss, family relations, stiffened gender relations, aging, resignation and death.

In general, life lessons might have a quality of everydayness, but Lillford's stories are funny, contrary, twisted and sometimes dark. There is nothing ordinary. Readers will quickly give up predicting how a story might end. Sudden changes in focus are smooth. A culprit might appear out of the blue. Characters are elegantly introduced, with so many layers, such detailed personalities. I appreciate how carefully these characters are crafted.

All these little details evoke authenticity and bring resonance. As a reader I am never told what to feel. Still the language in which the characters are introduced, in its precision, introduces in me emotion and opportunity for reflection.

I recommend paying attention to the first sentences of the stories: these are always a treasure. One of the most memorable ones, to me, is in 'Crystal Falls'. It is, however, unfair to mention just one.

Why did Daniel ask me to write this preface? Anthropologists and writers have much to talk about. We inhabit and appreciate similar worlds. Our work requires an attention to, and ability to recount, what at first might appear to be mere details of peoples' lifeworlds.

Both in my personal world and in my professional life, do I think about small places, often with long histories, that are unique, but also recognizably and often painfully entangled in larger world phenomena. Some of these places appear similar, in Norway, England, Canada, Australia.

Being a writer and an anthropologist might not be so different. We see some of the same things: otherwise-invisible heroes; traces in landscapes indicating past lives; the place of the sea in the histories of Northern peoples; the collaborative work of families over decades, and sometimes centuries, in the shaping of small communities.

There is also a difference. Daniel Lillford writes with a precision, a presence, an awareness of complexities of feelings, and with a great sense of humour. This I envy, and appreciate having in my life. It is a gift.

For me, to introduce this collection of short stories is an opportunity to pass this gift on.

G.B. Ween, Professor of Anthropology,
Museum of Cultural History, University of Oslo

For

John Dunsworth, a brilliant actor and the most generous, kindest man I have ever known.

and

Uncle Ian, who brought much happiness, friendship and wisdom into our little world in the cove, all those years ago.

These are works of fiction. The author has created the characters, conversations, interactions, and events; and any resemblance of any character to any real person is coincidental.

Contents

Foreword...3
1: The chicken catcher...9
2: The cut..19
3: Swifts in the rafters..35
4: The box..38
5: The light in the dunes..58
6: Burg's day..68
7: Crystal Falls...77
8: Selma..81
9: One Sunday...91
10: Roads back..101
11: Echo..107
12: Pink...113
13: The woods...123
14: The course...131
15: Red carnations...143
16: A better life...151
17: The longship..161
18: The truck...178
19: The promise...196
20: Davey and the dolphin..199
    Author's note..205
    Acknowledgements...207
    About the illustrator..208
    About the author..209

Daniel Lillford

1: The chicken catcher

The nameless woman on the phone said to meet the van by 7:30 am in the parking lot at the Tim Horton's, New Minas. She said they'd wait ten or so minutes, no more.

"Wear old clothes, bring some gloves. It's dirty work."

Dirty work. John Lamont grimaced at the memory, at the woman's nonchalance as he turned the key in the ignition. He wanted to smile, to somehow be above it all, but the sarcasm he felt would not crease his mouth with even a hint of joy.

It was still dark when a beaten-up twelve-seater Chevy van crawled into the parking lot with its lights on, slowed, and sat idling. John saw some dark figures get out of parked cars, hooded and hunched against the cold November morning, making their way toward the van. Two greasy individuals sat up front; both looked as if they'd kept away from water for a month of Sundays. Both were smoking. The bored passenger didn't even acknowledge his presence.

John said, "Is this the chicken catcher van?"

The driver looked him over. "You got it, bud. What's your name?"

He checked John's name off his list, a coffee-stained computer print-out on a clipboard. "Hop on board." The driver smiled, one gold tooth shone.

John climbed inside and almost keeled over from the stench of cigarette smoke, locker room sweat, and chicken shit. The floor was caked in it.

A girl, about 20, was sitting in the middle seats. She had a friendly smile. They exchanged pleasantries as the driver put the Chevy into gear and it grumbled out of the lot.

"What does a chicken catcher do?" he asked her.

"Never done it before?"

"No."

"Nothin' to it really. We just move the birds from cage to cage. You'll see. Money's good. Shitty work, though. Gets hot, dusty. But you'll get used to it."

Two in the back seat laughed.

"Some do, some don't," said the ferret-faced one with the AC/DC hoodie.

His eyes were red-rimmed and puffy. *Kid took a toke before coming to work*, John thought. He had pot-smoker's eyes.

The guy sitting beside him looked like an ex-jailbird, crude tats all over his arms and a thoughtful, little, perforated cut-line around his throat. He lit up a smoke and smiled, exposing a train wreck of rotting teeth and receding gums.

John wondered what he had signed on to as the driver slowed down and picked up two more passengers.

A young man climbed in, looking like he'd been in a recent fistfight. He swore as he lumped himself down beside the girl, then lit up a smoke, spat on the floor, swore again.

The other passenger, an older black man, got on quietly, sat down, very dignified, said nothing. It seemed like he wanted to be left alone. Had 'keep off the grass' written all over him. He caught no eye, just stared out of the filthy windows, contained in his thoughts. *Fair enough*, thought John.

Fields flashed by as the van moved out of the burbs and into the sunrise. It was a bad time to be on the patch, constantly fanning cigarette smoke away from his face. *Where is Gold Tooth taking us?*

He could see no houses, no more lights, they were driving deeper into the countryside. *Somewhere out Canning way*, he thought.

The girl kept up a constant monologue which revolved, mostly, around her boyfriend, who was at home somewhere and probably still asleep. She was friendly, but after fifteen minutes of mundanity, John wished she'd just be quiet and enjoy the scenery. Boring prattle was annoying at any time, but always worse first thing in the morning.

The large grey silos of a factory farm loomed into view and the van geared down. *So this is it.*

The van moved up a rut-muddied track, then stopped beside a steel hangar the size of a small battleship. It was hard to take in at first. John had never seen a structure like this one before.

Another van arrived with more chicken catchers, mostly women in this crew. Middle-aged, many lined faces, lifeless brittle hair, more smokers. Some were dressed in what could only be called rags. Hard tickets, all of them.

The Chevy door swung open and stale cigarette smoke wafted into the countryside as the chicken catchers grumbled, spat, swore, and fumbled into the light. John looked across the empty fields and breathed deeply. It was the last breath of fresh air he was going to get for some time. *Where are we? What is this place?*

Gold Tooth unlocked the shed door, and one by one the chicken catchers moved inside. The nauseating smell of ammonia filled up John's nose, giving him an instant headache.

The black man glanced at John. But if he was smiling, it was hard to tell. He was already wearing a protective white face mask. *Smart man*, John thought, as he gave him a friendly nod. But the old guy remained silent, aloof from the group.

Gold Tooth, the foreman, the driver, whatever his true title, told them they were moving 5,000 birds from one part of the factory to the other side of the factory. If this seemed a pointless exercise, nobody asked why, and no explanation was given.

All he said was, "Just get this fucking nightmare over with, and we should be done before lunch."

This seemed to please quite a few of the crew. Gold Tooth handed John a protective paper mask, slightly used. "You'll need this."

He walked away looking at his clipboard. John looked at the stained mask. It was better than nothing.

A door rolled open, long chains clanking. Someone switched the overhead lights on. And there it was: Stalag Leghorn.

The sound of chickens squawking and cackling filled the hangar to a deafening pitch. Yellow-beaked heads poked out of line upon

11

line upon line of metal cages, white feathers jammed tight against the sides with little if any room to move. Eight, sometimes ten birds per cage.

The hangar was long: a ten-minute walk from one end to the other. Aisles of chickens, all squawking, backed up like a blocked sewer. The aisles between the cages were barely wide enough for the trolleys. One thing was certain, you couldn't work in this place if you were fat. This was a lean machine. Every inch was accounted for. Efficiency plus. John wondered who could design such a corporate hell.

Then the trolleys started to roll across the floors. Some started mid-section, others at either end. Cages were opened, then chickens were manhandled by the catchers, grabbed by the legs, two at a time in each hand, then taken from the stationary cages and brutally stuffed into the trolley cages.

John was trying to be gentle with the hens as they flapped about, obviously distressed, picking them up like he used to when he had his own chickens on the farm. On the farm....He tried not to think about it. This was not that world. *Forget about it, John, forget about it.*

As he was new, he was slow and holding up production. He was blessed to be working with someone experienced, and a real prize piece of humanity: an expletive-frothing hunchback, who couldn't have been more than 21, but who looked 35. His face was long and pale, blotchy in places where pimples erupted, and eyes that were dark, hard to read. His lank hair was greasy and dandruff flakes sat on his black hoodie like a sprinkling of baby powder. Stale sweat emanated from his clothing, and when he talked it sounded like he had a permanent runny nose.

But he knew everything there was to know about this "fucking" business. The oracle of Notre Damnation, no less.

At first, trying to be friendly, John asked, "How long have you been doing this job?'

Aggressively, quite out of the blue and for no obvious reason, Hunchy said, "I pull in four hundred fucking bucks a week, and I'm fucking proud of that."

Then he asked John how much he made in a week, grinning like he already knew the answer to his question. He didn't wait for John to respond. He didn't have to, because he knew who the chicken catchers were and why most of them were here.

He, on the other hand, was different. He was a regular. He liked this job. They always called him in first. That was the difference. The difference between a regular and a fucking blow-in.

Then, for reasons best known to himself, Hunchy decided to tell John about his medical history. He wasn't a well man: he had heart problems.

Working here in this health spa, John thought, *surely not?* Still, four hundred bucks was four hundred bucks, the ammonia, the dust, and all the shit aside, so who was he to point out why the hunchback might be sick? Besides that, why should he care? Like two animals that meet, circling, sniffing the air, gauging each other's strengths, weaknesses, John and Hunchy disliked each other almost immediately.

They never exchanged names. That would be too familiar. Perhaps it was his age, maybe it was the questions he asked, his accent, John didn't know. He just knew that the day was going to be longer than he'd anticipated.

~

Cage after cage after cage, birds flapping, some flying away; the pecking, the cursing, the dirt and the stench; perhaps worst of all, the proximity of blind ignorance in leadership. *No, John, this is not the time to start up a discussion on the merits of George Orwell's* Animal Farm. *Not here. Wrong audience, pal.*

John gritted his teeth behind the paper mask, smiled at his thoughts all the same. Maybe the ludicrous would help him through this nightmare.

What conversation there was between the two men was strained, filtered at best. It became even worse when Hunchy started reaching for birds in cages above John's head. There was little enough room as it was, and now it was becoming dangerous. John had already ducked a few times as Hunchy's birds descended, flapping past his face to be stuffed roughly into the trolley cages below.

And then it happened. He wasn't quick enough. One of the leghorn's claws cut across his cheek, just below the left eye.

John felt the sharp pain of the cut and had to hold himself back from lashing out. He knew instinctively that Hunchy had done this on purpose, to put this old fart in his place, but of course he couldn't prove that.

Instead, he told the hunchback in words he rarely ever used to watch what he was doing and to be more careful. The cold look in John Lamont's sea-grey eyes made it perfectly clear that a line had been drawn. *Medical condition or not, cross that line pal, and you will suffer the consequences.*

Hunchy begrudgingly got the drift and moved further up the aisle, muttering and cursing to himself as he went. No apology escaped his lips.

John touched his cheek and felt the angry scratch swelling up. It was then that he noticed he'd already taken his gloves off.

Normally a cheerful and thoughtful man, a man not predisposed to violence, he hadn't felt like punching anyone in the face since high school. But he quietly relished the idea of it now.

Perhaps Hunchy sensed it. He kept his distance.

After a few more cages of gentleness, John, too, became rougher with the inmates. He hated himself for what he was doing, but he was now stuffing those miserable wretches into the trolley cages just as hard and as fast as the catcher working beside him. Trying to keep up. To do this job. Business. Efficiency. Never personal. It couldn't be. These things weren't meant to have names. Why, even the cages were numberless. They were just "the five thousand." Nobody appeared to care. Nobody had time to give it a second thought.

John didn't want to think about the birds, either. But he did. Over the course of an hour, John watched the catchers stuff the birds in ass-backwards, upside down, flattened them in to make more room, one bird on top of another. *What if a wing gets broken in the process?*

He asked that question. Hunchy looked at John as if he were a moron. Didn't he know where these birds ended up?

And with each bird John stuffed into a cage he felt more and more like a miserable excuse for a human being. They were just chickens. And this was just getting a dirty job done, that was all there was to it. *Wise up, John. Just get 'er done. You're nothing but one link in this glorious little operational chain, just another wrangler following orders, getting "the five thousand" through to their next stop. A small part of the treadmill before they reach their final station, the fast food restaurants' deep fat fryers. And nobody working in here today gives a flying fuck about broken wings, broken necks, or twisted, upside-down birds in overflowing cages. It doesn't matter. They don't matter.*

Hundreds of eggs lay in the now-empty aisle cages, white and small, brittle, undernourished. Many were broken. Their yokes were an insipid yellow dripping from cage to cage and then down onto the concrete floor. Small pools of watery custard lying in the muck and the dust. *Always a sign of a poorly-fed chicken and typical of factory produce.*

He knew. He'd had a farm once, before the bank took it away. His hens laid healthy eggs. But he had maintained healthy animals, unlike this obscenity he found himself involved with now.

Occasionally a dead bird lay under the feet of its cellmates. John thought these birds were the lucky ones. Their torture was over.

Some chickens made a valiant dash for freedom. They'd flap out of a catcher's gloves, squawking loudly, dirt and feathers going everywhere, whirling through the caustic air. A futile exercise, because there was nowhere for them to hide in this barracks of efficiency. Some managed to roost on the overhanging lights, but most were caught quickly, then back to the trolleys, the cages, into the hands of the guards who were making 12 bucks an hour to work where no self-respecting soul ought to work.

During the smoke break—most of the catchers smoked—John looked around the countryside, breathing in the good clean air again, wishing he had brought a thermos, if only to take the taste of

Daniel Lillford

the factory from his mouth.

He studied the faces, priding himself on being a reasonable judge of character. For many in this motley crew this was the last refuge. Perhaps their last chance. A place for the poor, the down-at-heel, the criminals, the addicts, the unwashed, the uneducated…the unloved. A subculture doing what nobody else could or would do.

One woman with a beige-coloured face, terribly lined, told John she'd been working at Larsen's meatpacking plant in Berwick for 25 years. That was before they shut it down and laid everyone off last month. "Nobody got a warning," she said. "Caught us all out….That's just what they did."

She had to get a job to feed her family, any job would do. She looked unhappy, hammered hard by life. But she was thankful to be working, even in this hellhole.

John watched her smoking her cigarette, small tight puffs. He felt sad for her. But there were no words. What could he say?

John knew about being poor. Wasn't he just the same as some of these sorry ones? *What use pride now, John?*

His conscience pricked and the scratch under his eye smarted. Still, here they all were, lording it over these birds, these awkward raptor-looking creatures, these beady-eyed monsters. These humble chickens.

More than once John had to bite his lip with Hunchy, who was engaged in cursing at the harmless birds as he stuffed and rammed their sorry carcasses into their trolley cages. He enjoyed his job and there was no doubt in John's mind that this creep had a twisted streak. He seemed to relish his power over the weak and the helpless like some grotesque medieval dungeon torturer.

John's eyes were burning terribly. Chicken shit covered everything. He'd thought that by being so busy the time would fly by. Not so in this place. One hour had dragged to feel like two.

And so it went on until they had moved 5,000 birds from cages to trolleys, then back to cages again. Pecked at, shat on, covered in dust, choked with ammonia, and worst of all, ear-bashed by a hunchback know-it-all, whose every sentence started and ended with an expletive.

They completed the task before midday arrived: four and a half hours that had felt like eight. John knew for certain that he looked like shit, because everybody else did. All the catchers looked like members of some weird platoon that had walked out of a war zone.

Before going back to the van, he took one last look at the rows and rows of model efficiency. A factory full of metal cages and their crammed, feathered occupants. The death rows…A vile place designed by some soulless prick. *Where does it start?* he thought. *Where does this cruelty begin? Where? Is it simply power? An efficient business model? Profit?*

One of the catchers called, "The van's about to leave."

The drive home was painful. His eyes were sore and ached, and his heart felt beaten up. He stank. Boy, did he stink.

He wanted to see his wife and children. To be home again. To wash it all away. But most of all he just felt like crying. It had come to this. 'Dirty work.' *Jeezus, you don't know the half of it.*

Home. John took the longest shower he'd ever had in his life. The town water rates could go to blazes. He needed to come back to civility. To be in the company of intelligent and caring people again. To feel kindness, know it existed, not to have to seek it out.

His eyes remained red and sore for days on end. Sleep was restless, painful, troubled. It was as if a teaspoon of grit lay underneath each lid.

He'd lasted less than half a day as a chicken catcher. But the smell of chickens stayed with him for weeks, like it was part of him now, in his pores…or deeper.

Daniel Lillford

2: The cut

People consider Bo Langille a lucky man for one reason and one reason only: he married Crystal Heisler.

As Larry Dauphinee will tell you, whether you wish to hear it or not, "If God could pour concrete the way Crystal Heisler pours herself into her jeans, then the big fella oughta be in the construction business. No three axe handles across the arse there, boys!"

Bo and Crystal have been happily married for four years, but their union remains a source of debate and gossip. Many still ask what the hell did a beauty like Crystal Heisler see in that great clod to want to marry him in the first place? Answers vary.

Iona McRae told Selma Dorey she'd heard Bo had a big one, big as a donkey.

Selma nodded whilst she fed Rex, her old Tom, a can of Brunswick herrings, and said, "Saw him when he was born. Had a right whopper. Even the nurse took a second look, yup. A real trout. Oh, but youse never saw such a homely baby...A face only a mother could love. Oh, my land, but he was an ugly baby, f'sure. Sad all the same, after nine long months that's what Effie Langille gets for all her troubles. Yup, sad."

"What I was just sayin'!" Iona said, smacking the gingham tablecloth to emphasize the point and sending a few Players butts out of the ashtray and onto the linoleum. Iona exercised the thought that Bo was not such a bad catch, that that Crystal Heisler was a smart one. All them Heislers were shrewd. After all, didn't Bo own his house and his boat, a Cape Islander, was fully paid off; he was a hard worker, a good fisherman, and he got the pogey in the off-season? Crystal was all set.

Okay, so Bo wasn't no Elvis—Iona's teen crush—but that's why they invented them light globes an' a wall switch. The dark can be a great comforter to a woman, especially when she has to look into the face of someone like Bo Langille.

Selma took this all in as she scratched Rex and looked for fleas. She caught one and cracked its back between her yellowed fingernails, adding maliciously, "Must be shootin' blanks all the same; nothing showin' in three years...An' everyone knows them Heisler women are as fertile as rabbits, so it ain't her."

Iona nodded knowingly.

And so it was agreed. Bo might possess a whopper, but he had no ammunition.

~

Whilst feeding mackerel into the tuna trap-nets set off Horse Island, Avery Cooke was telling Daniel Murphy his thoughts on the Langille-Heisler marriage. He limped with his gimpy hip from the mackerel box, scattering shovelfuls of the half-frozen fish into the pen to entice the big blue fins up to the surface.

"Face like the arse-end of a horse havin' a shit...What she sees in him, God only knows...Sumpthin' goin' on there, that's f'sure, yup, that's f'sure...Man hit pay dirt with that woman, knows that. Must be getting' poontang mornin', noon, an' night. Knows I would be! I'd be givin' it to her every chance I'd get, all day till me pecker got sore an' fell off!"

"Jealous?" Dan said.

"Jealous!?" he laughed. "Well, yes sir, f'sure! Wouldn't youse be?"

Dan smirked, but didn't answer. He was used to Avery blowing hard, wishing for kisses, winning the lottery, anything he thought that would make his life better.

The yellow spines of the big fish were moving closer toward the surface, hungrier now.

"But youse gotta ask yourself what she sees in him, eh? An' what she sees in him must be only sumpthin' *she* sees in him. That's women for youse, Dan'll, an' that's a fact."

Avery scattered more mackerel with the shovel, watching the

large fish darting beneath the seine boat, which was rocking from side to side as more blue-fin joined in the feeding.

"Must have a cock like a bull, Dan'll, cock like a bull f'sure, yup. Big ole' Babe Ruth…Yup, that's a fact."

Dan mouthed 'That's a fact' as he watched one tuna they'd christened Old Smokey, at least 800 lbs, slash and thrash through the water, chewing up seven or eight large mackerel in one gulp.

"Fella I knew once got his hand bit by a tuna, yup. Made him bleed like a stuck pig. Helluva nasty gash…yup…What she sees in him Dan'll, God only knows."

Avery shook his head. Dan looked at Avery, and shook his head, too.

~

Normally Bo'd drive down the hill, but the other morning he had walked past Dan's house looking like a man with the weight of an anchor dragging down his shoulders. Dan noticed he hadn't shaved, that his eyes looked tired, sort of sad today. His big lumbering frame trudged one rubber boot after the other as if he were a Clydesdale pulling a wagon load of beer.

"Mornin', Bo!" Dan said, as he cupped his coffee between his hands.

Bo turned and gave Dan the hundred-yard stare, half touched his ball cap, then continued onward. If he said, "Mornin', Dan," it was in a whisper, and Dan never heard him. It wasn't hard to see a man with trouble on his mind.

He watched Bo walk down to the government wharf and climb aboard his boat, disappearing below deck. It was choppy out there. Neptune's horses were running amok and the small fishing fleet was going nowhere. Not today.

It was a strange, overcast day for August; it looked like rain was coming, but Dan could usually feel rain in his bones, and today he couldn't feel a blessed thing.

He watched the light in Bo's wheelhouse flick into life. *Must be doing some repairs.*

Daniel Lillford

When word reached Luke Boutilier that Crystal had left Bo the night before, his first reaction was, "Go on!?" If he showed surprise, inside he only felt an old annoying ache.

Larry Dauphinee, the messenger, was grinning like a troll with nicotine stained teeth. "What goes 'round, comes 'round. Youse jest have to wait your turn, Lukey-boy! Bitch'll soon be in heat again."

Luke stared at the chuckling troll, taking in Larry's bat-like features. Here was a man he'd never really taken to, never had much time for. Often, in company, Luke would call Larry, behind his back, a gossipin' old sonofabitch. He kept his distance from Larry, as did most of his fishermen buddies. Larry was there to be tolerated, like the village idiot.

Besides, any fisherman around here who drove a Japanese car didn't get much respect. Larry drove a beige Datsun, known locally as 'The Shitty Dat'.

Still, in their gruff, hard way, most of the fishermen felt a little sorry for the poor, sex-starved bastard. Everyone suspected, or claimed to know, that Larry's first-born, Willard, wasn't his. Larry's estranged wife Mary-Ellen, before she became the north side of a house, was quite attractive in a heavy-set kind of way; and there was no doubt she'd played the field in her youth. But after Willard was born, Mary-Ellen decided she liked it on the couch with her daytime soaps and her packets of chips, and that was where she was going to stay. Like a mushroom in the darkness, she just kept on growing and growing.

Larry sleeps in the family fish shack across the road with his Jack Russell terrier and 14 years of *Hustler* magazines, dreaming about women he'll never know and could never afford. He hasn't said a word to his wife in over 15 years. Mary-Ellen seems content with this arrangement.

Luke continued to work on his boat engine, but his mind was back at an old high-school dance in 1984. A girl was dancing the night away to a Simple Minds song. She was the most beautiful girl he'd ever seen. Larry was still talking rubbish, but Luke wasn't listening, he was remembering the one that got away; Crystal Heisler.

~

Iona McRae had watched Crystal through her grandmother's binoculars from the safety of her kitchen window. She was following in a long family tradition. She'd seen Crystal drive up to her mother's old place, seen her lugging suitcases off the back of the Dodge, taking them inside the old Cape Cod that hadn't been lived in since Mrs. Heisler had passed on some five years before.

Iona cherished a grim smile across her down-turned mouth as her mind leapt into her favourite territory: speculation! In the time it took for Crystal to close the front door and turn on the hall light, Iona was already dialing Selma's number. It was 10.35 pm.

"Selma, you'll never guess what I jest seen…"

Crystal put the suitcases in the middle of the parlour. She moved into the kitchen, turned on the light, found the kettle, filled it and set it on the ancient range. She breathed heavily, an exasperated exhale, as if something unspeakably angry was trying to rise from her gut and yell blue murder into the world. Then she breathed again, slowly, gently, simmering, controlling.

Her eyes took in the turquoise-painted walls, the cherry-stained cedar wainscotting, the pine cupboards, a spotless kitchen bench with steel canisters marked Flour, Sugar, Coffee, Tea, all in order like guardsmen glinting on parade. They had always looked like that. Her mom's kitchen had been her place of pride and joy, and the old lady sure knew how to cook. For the briefest moment Crystal saw her mom again, sleeves rolled up, flour sprinkled over the wooden table, rolling pastry for her blueberry pies, prize-winners at fairs and church socials.

Bo had wanted her to sell her mom's house, but Crystal couldn't. It was her family home, her childhood. She loved the old place and still spent time there when the world pressed a little too close.

A fly buzzed and pinged against the window. She was glad it wasn't a bee; she didn't like bees in the house. Bad luck to kill bees in the house. They had to be caught, taken outside and released.

The yellow swatter took care of the bluebottle. She washed its guts down the sink.

Now it was quiet, only a breeze rattling one of the upstairs bedroom windows. Probably her mother's old room. The house was over 150 years old and solid, and it would still be standing when all the modern ones were piled up in dust. She'd tried to convince Bo to move in, but he wasn't interested. No Langille boy ever moved into his wife's home. Some things weren't done. Not in this neck of the woods. People would talk. They did anyway, but not about that.

She made her way upstairs, turned left at the landing and opened her bedroom door. The bottom hinge still creaked. A 1940s single sleigh bed nestled underneath the window. Shelving on one side was bursting with her well-thumbed childhood favourites: *Emily of New Moon, Black Beauty, Gone with the Wind, The House at Pooh Corner, The Lion, the Witch and the Wardrobe, The Magic Faraway Tree*. A collection of Barbie dolls filled a middle shelf, many with brightly coloured Mohawks—a rebellious stage in her youth.

A poster of the 80's pop stars Duran-Duran was taped above her vanity mirror and dresser. She smiled as she lingered on the made-up faces of these androgynous boys. She'd once had a crush on Simon Le Bon, the lead singer, and used to dream about him. But she never told her mom about those dreams. She never told her mom she masturbated thinking about Simon Le Bon. Sitting heavily on the bright patchwork quilt that covered the bed, her long dark hair fell over her face as she stared at the floorboards. She wanted to cry, but somehow…

The kettle started to scream, and she wished she hadn't put it on. She didn't want a cup of tea anyway…Habit. Her mother had always done that: she'd come in, no matter what time of day, and the first thing she did was head for the kitchen, put the kettle on, make a pot of tea…

Habit…Was she turning into her mom? Jeezus…She thought about Bo and wished she could reverse the night. But she couldn't, and in the pit of her stomach she felt she was a goddamn fool.

~

Dan Murphy was taking his nightly constitutional down to the wharf with his dog Bluey, a lab-collie mix. He'd been watching Bo's boat on and off for most of the day. The light in the wheelhouse was still burning. It was 10 pm.

Bluey sauntered ahead of him, sniffing every guard-rail post, cocking his leg for seconds, then moving on. Dan knew Bluey wouldn't stray too far.

He turned on to the wharf and walked to Bo's Cape Islander, where he stood for a few moments, watching and listening. The sea rocked the moored boats, a lullaby sea, the gentle snoring of buoys and rubber tires pushing against the woodwork moving with the night.

Dan could see no sign of Bo, but he knew he was there. He glanced up to see where Bluey had got to and spotted him heading up the hill toward Lily Coolen's place. She often threw table scraps out for the gulls, and Bluey was hoping for an extra feed.

Dan smiled, put his foot on the Cape's prow. "Are you in there, Bo?"

He received no answer, but was sure he heard the roll of a bottle, something chinking.

When he got to the wheelhouse he found Bo sitting on the floor cradling a 12-gauge pump action. There were three pints of Captain Morgan rum beside him, two empty.

It was the shotgun that concerned Dan. "Too dark to go shootin' at seals, Bo..."

Bo nodded slowly, said nothing.

Dan got closer, squatted to be eye-level with him. He saw that Bo's eyes were bloodshot, sad, and if he had to guess, he'd say the man had been crying. Maybe for hours. Maybe all day.

Dan reached over very gently, took the shotgun from Bo's lap, and put the firearm against a wall, glancing in the breech. It was primed.

Bo's voice was thick, like molasses. "Wasn't goin' to do anythin' stoopid, Dan...jest...jest thinkin', is all."

Dan took out a pack of cigarettes, offered one to Bo, who took it and let it hang off the edge of his lips like a train hanging off a blown bridge. They smoked and said nothing in the time it takes to smoke a Players.

"Heard Seldon's crew got a few more tuna in their trap yesterday."

Bo nodded like a man who couldn't care less.

"He's havin' a good year so far. That makes seven in the one trap, not too shabby. Reckon he'll show up with a new truck, end of the season, you see if he don't."

Bo stubbed the smoke out on the floor with his gigantic thumb. He took another swig at the jug, then offered it to Dan, who declined the invitation.

He could hear Bluey skipping along the road, searching for its master. Dan whistled and heard his dog's paws quicken as they approached the wharf, then stop as he sniffed outside Bo's boat.

"Gotta a good dawg there, Dan... Good dawg... I oughta get a good dawg."

Dan smiled, agreed.

~

Bo liked Dan Murphy. Dan was the strong, quiet type. Bo never heard him bad-mouth anyone. He worked hard, and he kept himself to himself. Dan looked like the actor Jimmy Stewart, or so Bo thought, but maybe he was getting him mixed up with Henry Fonda.

Crystal was the one who had noticed that. She was the movies fan. She liked old movies. *Twelve Angry Men*, wasn't that one of her favourites?

Dan reminded Bo a little of his father, who had died of a heart attack while hauling in mackerel nets. Bo missed his father. Sometimes he would pretend his old man was still alive and have whispered conversations with him when he was out hunting.

Bo never built tree stands like so many of the men around here did. He called those kinds of hunters "Oswalds", bushwhackers he had no respect for, regardless of their posturing, their manliness, those silly orange vests and hats they all wore. Any fool could put a bag of Macintosh apples under a tree, sit in a stand opposite, drink beer and wait for a deer to show. Nothing about hunting in that. Assassination, no more nor less.

Hunting was the closest thing to a philosophy Bo would ever have, though to his way of thinking it was nothing more than common sense, simple survival and above all, personal pride. Bo liked to wake up around 3 am in the season, and when he had breakfasted and gotten ready, he was out of his house half an hour later. He'd walk straight into the woods, always quietly, always listening. When he was a boy his father had tied a neckerchief around his mouth. He wasn't allowed to talk, and the neckerchief taught him how to breathe gentler, to move quieter.

From moss rock to moss rock, staying off the leaves. It was all about patience, listening and keeping your eyes open.

Every year since he'd turned nine, he'd brought a deer out of the woods. And his father made him carry the first one he ever shot, a three-rack buck, for half a mile before he gave the boy a hand.

His father had been a tough task master, a real hard-nose, a man not many would stand to cross. But Bo had loved his old man and deeply respected him. The last time he had cried was when he held his father in his arms in the green seine boat where he died. Bo was right beside him when it happened.

His father's last words were, "Well, I'll be fucked..." And that was that, eleven years ago.

Bo had been thinking about a cougar he'd seen last year. He'd watched her with her cub not more than 30 yards away from where he was standing. She'd licked her cub, then lifted her nose into the wind.

The government "experts" said there weren't any Eastern cougars left in these woods, but Bo knew that was a steaming dollop. He'd seen two in as many years and tracks in mud and snow years before that. He never told anyone, because sure as hell some fool'd try and get himself a pelt. There were enough killers out there drinking beer whilst waiting in their old lawn chairs stuck up in the trees.

In between memories of his father and the animals he'd seen,

Crystal's face had moved through his thoughts like a ghost, as if she were turning the pages of a favourite comic book... He loved her more than he knew how to say.

Some men have that gift, they can talk, they know words, good words...Bo knew how useless he was at expressing anything that meant anything from deep inside himself.

Knowing she wasn't in their home filled his heart with emptiness, it made his chest heavy. Perhaps if he'd been more of an enlightened man, an educated man, he mightn't have lost his temper and thrown her out. He might, had he been better educated, more enlightened, have tried to listen to her, tried to understand. But like the weather-worn bullhead that he was, all he had heard was that she had kissed another man.

She told him so herself. Brazenly, so he thought. And all he could do was react violently, grabbing her by the back of her hair and the belt in her jeans, throwing her out onto the porch, slamming the door, then grabbing clothes and suitcases, throwing them out one after another in a minor hurricane of broken-hearted fury.

If he had been a gentler, kinder man, he mightn't have called her a whore...but he did. If he never meant it, he shouldn't have said it. He also knew that pride was his monkey. His father had given him that...and for a moment he hated the old man's guts.

~

Crystal was staring at the fading light casting shadows across Duran-Duran. Simon Le Bon was beginning to look macabre, like some evil Chucky doll.

Why had she kissed Jamie Nauss at the mill Christmas party? Why had she allowed him the liberty of slipping his hand into her blouse and fondling her breasts? At least she was wearing a bra.

Why, after eight long months of feeling guilty, had she decided to confess her indiscretion to her husband? Did she expect anything different from Bo? Why had she waited so long? Was she frightened of Bo, or just frightened of herself? And why, why hadn't she just kept her big mouth shut? She should have just let sleeping dogs lie and lived with it.

Her mother's favourite lines were, "Honesty is the best policy, Crystal dear. You'll always feel better for telling the truth. Your conscience will be clear. God will smile and love you all the more..."

She spoke quietly to the ceiling. "Honesty can be a crock, mom."

Jamie Nauss was just a boy, ten years younger than herself. She had 30 to look forward to in October. She knew why she had kissed him: he looked a little like Simon Le Bon, the blonde hair, that grin...He reminded her of her past. He was young, full of dreams, always smiling. Only last month he'd left to seek his fortune in Vancouver. She wouldn't see him at the mill any more.

She would miss him. When he came into the office it was like he brought fair weather in with him. He made her feel light, breezy, and he liked talking about films like she did. He read, too. He was always telling her about this book and that book, an article he'd read...

Bo read the local paper, *The Clipper*, and that was about it. In all the years she'd known him, she'd never seen him pick up a book, unless it was to swat some insect, and when he threw her Oxford dictionary at a raccoon that had walked into their kitchen.

At the office party, she was the one who had suggested they step outside to look at the stars. She was responsible. Things just got a little out of hand. It could have happened to anyone, any married...person.

It wasn't as if they'd had sex. She hadn't touched him. Not like that.

But in her heart, she knew that she wanted to, and she'd had to fight herself off, as well as the soft, gentle hands of a younger man who had wanted her.

She didn't tell Bo about Jamie fondling her breasts; never had the time. Probably just as well. All she remembered was his eyes darkening, a terrible cloudiness coming over him. It was like watching a storm roll in. And then he was hauling her out of the house, pitching her into the night. He'd called her a whore, her own husband...

"Is that what I am, mom?"

Her eyes started to get heavy. She still hadn't cried. She wondered if Bo would remember to defrost the freezer; it needed cleaning out.

~

Bluey led the way up Miller's Hill, glancing back every minute or so to make sure Dan was following, which he was whilst trying to prop up a lurching wreck. Dan had talked Bo into going home to sleep it off after a few hours of listening to half-finished sentences about hunting, fishing and "stoopid eejits." Not once had Bo mentioned Crystal. He didn't have to.

Dan knew that if things had been good between them and Bo was just on another of his benders, which occurred every eight weeks or so, Crystal would already be out looking for him in the Dodge. And, as she had done so often before, she would have piled the sorry lump into the passenger side and taken him home and put him to bed in the spare room, the one she'd always wanted for the nursery. Still, Dan kept his eyes open for truck lights, hoping.

The only car that passed them was young Sharon Meisner's hotted up Jetta. You could hear the beat-box from that thing coming a mile off. Some called it 'The Rap-Crapper'.

Nope, Crystal wouldn't be looking for Bo, not tonight.

Bo was walking slower than he usually walked. He'd slipped a few knots as he held on to Dan's shoulder to steady himself. Dan could feel his shifting weight and smell the stale alcohol and cigarettes.

"You're a good man, Dan...the very best."

He had said that three times and they hadn't yet walked fifty yards. The dog had stopped and waited so they could catch up.

Bo stopped, queasy, and looked out at the blinking lights reflecting across the cove. They were just past Dan's house now. "Beautiful...ain't she, eh Dan?"

"Are you talkin' 'bout the Cove or your wife, Bo?"

Bo began to speak, then went pale and started to heave all over the guard rail. Dan made a note of where and glanced at Bluey, who was also taking note.

There are few sorrier sights than a grown man spilling out his drunken guts. Every mouthful represents something: Joy, misery, sentiment, remorse, love, longing, guilt. It's always a stinking mess. Always a waste.

Bo wiped his mouth with his greasy plaid shirt sleeve, stared across the water and said nothing.

After a minute Dan said, "No sign'a Crystal in the truck yet."

Bo shook his head. "She ain't comin'. I...I kicked her out. Whorin'...Youse know..."

Dan didn't, and he didn't believe Crystal was a whore either.

"She'll be at her mom's old house...yup...that's where she'll be."

Bo belched. Dan nodded, took out another cigarette and lit up.

"Why'd youse never git married, Dan?"

The question surprised Dan, its directness, but he didn't show anything. "Never met the right one I guess," he said carelessly.

Bo studied Dan for a moment, his bloodshot eyes searching. Then he gulped and left a rum cocktail over a spruce sapling.

Dan had lied. Maybe Bo knew that when he looked into his eyes for that brief moment.

Dan had met the right one once, but that was many moons ago. At 43 he had no interest in hanging around in bars or attending church socials. For one thing, he didn't drink, not any more. Second, he wasn't sure about God, though he did like Jesus.

When he lay on his bed gently scratching behind Bluey's ears, Dan often felt the twinge in his left knee that would forever remind him of what a lethal Molotov cocktail a fast car, alcohol and a girlfriend without a seat belt can be. Screeching tires would forever make him shudder, and some nights he woke up smelling gasoline, with the taste of blood in his mouth.

When Crystal went around to try to talk things over, the house was locked up and dark. Bo wasn't there. On the porch she found her stuff neatly packed up in wooden fish-boxes and her collection of snow domes jumbled into a Keith's beer box along with the framed wedding photographs.

Her most sentimental snow dome, Santa in his sleigh flying

through the air over an idyllic village, was cracked and leaking. It had been a small gift from her father the Christmas before he had run off to Alberta with Evelyn Croucher, 16 years his junior. Crystal was 12 at the time. It was the last present he had given her with his own hands.

Afterwards, when he remembered her birthday, he sent the occasional ten dollar bill in a cheap syrupy drug-store card. Over the years she'd given up expecting a birthday card, ten bucks or a Christmas card, cheap or otherwise. Last she heard he was living in Drumheller and had found God. Sure needed to find something.

She put her belongings in the Dodge and drove away, tossing the snow dome out of the window into the ditch.

~

Crystal went to Halifax, got her hair done and came back with a bob. Iona said you could tell it wasn't cut locally, the lines were too straight and there were no highlights.

Bo disconnected the phone. He had started living in his camp up along the Mersey River, a shack he used in trout season. It wasn't much, but he didn't need much, not any more. He four-wheeled in and out and still got down to his boat at 4 am before anyone else was around.

Bo's brother, Jesse, was helping him out with the bluefin trap, and Dan sometimes worked for him when an extra hand was required.

Dan kept a careful watch on Bo at first, but as September moved onward he was less inclined to hang around at the end of the working day, preferring the company of his dog and his jazz records, leaving Bo and Jesse to drink by themselves, talk their nonsense.

Summer rolled into fall, hunting season came round again. The maples had turned the forest carpet the colour of fire. Days were crisp, cloudless and still.

Crystal liked walking the old logging road back of St. Cuthbert's Anglican church, where she had been baptized. She wore her hunter-orange hat just in case some of the "Oswalds" were about and took her for a deer. You never knew. She'd ducked for cover more than once before. And she was always careful not to wear her white Levis.

Today was her birthday, October 24th. Four years before, in a small clearing up ahead, as they sat on a flat rock, Bo Langille had proposed to her and she had accepted. She remembered how proper and sweet he'd been that day, how his words were plain spoken and gentle, not mumbled or blurred, as if he'd been practising for a week. He had, and he'd consumed much in preparation.

He had looked big and strong, like a bear. His eyes were kind. She could always stare into his eyes and know that he would love her forever.

A year later they were married in an uncomplicated ceremony down on Bayswater Beach. Bo had looked handsome, albeit uncomfortable, in a dark blue suit he never wore again. It had been a happy day. She was a happy bride. That memory made her sad now.

~

Bo felt the bruise on his jaw and smiled through the ache. He was glad Dan Murphy had hit him, socked him a good one and knocked him over. He'd lain on the ground looking up at Dan wondering why.

Well, Dan had told him sure enough. "You're An ignorant, belligerent, backward, unforgiving bonehead who wouldn't know a good thing if it came up and bit you on your friggin' arse!"

Dan sure was pissed. Those were big words he was hollering. He'd never seen the man so riled.

Then Dan had reached into his jacket and pulled out a six-week-old pup, a black and white mongrel with tan front paws. He'd thrust it at Bo and said, "Here! Have a good dog, seein' as you don't want a good wife."

His friend left Bo lying on the wharf, with the puppy licking his bewildered face.

Daniel Lillford

Now he felt its warmth inside his jacket. It was sleeping, its little head resting between the middle buttons. The whole morning in the woods the pup had been quiet, hardly a peep.

When Bo spotted a large buck, five-rack at least, he levelled his rifle with practised ease. It was then the pup sneezed and the buck bolted.

Crystal scuffed the fallen leaves as her boots trod a well-worn path toward the clearing. She was so deep in her thoughts that she didn't even feel the presence of Bo walking not 15 feet to her right along mossy rocks, his rifle slung across his camouflage jacket.

On the flat rock ahead, where he had proposed, lay a bunch of violets and a greeting card he'd bought from the drugstore. Inside it read:

> Happy Birthday. I'm sorry.
> Please come home.
> I love you, Bo.

The lettering was big, childlike and clumsy. Just like him. Crystal read it and burst into tears.

Bo watched silently. The last time he'd seen her cry was on their wedding day. He'd wondered then if she wasn't having second thoughts. Tears always meant sadness in his family, nothing else.

He looked away. He wanted to hold her. He wondered why she'd cut her hair.

The pup sneezed.

3: Swifts in the rafters

The old man stood in the barn, but he couldn't remember why he'd walked up from the woodlot to be here now. He stared at his workbench as if the collection of well-ordered tools hanging on the wall could give him an answer.

"Another brain fart, Jimbo...Jeezus..."

The collie sat by its master and let loose a gentle whine. He patted the dog's head as it leaned its body closer into his legs. He looked down at his rough-veined hand, concentrating hard. Maybe the hand itself would point him in the right direction.

In his mind he went back to what it was he had been doing before trudging the hundred yards from woodlot to barn, thinking to himself, *Why can't I remember? Why did I come in here?*

The sound of a whirring chainsaw, flying chips and images of falling logs thudding into the sawdust around the sawhorse filled his head. He was thinking hard. The chainsaw suddenly cut out. Then he smiled.

Half-whistling to himself, he made his way across the barn to the shelving behind the old John Deere tractor. He found the chainsaw oil alongside paint cans and a Jerry can of gasoline. His fingers were shaking as he lifted the oil container and moved back to the work bench. He paused, his brow creasing like a road map.

The dog lay down on the stained wide floorboards and looked up, as always, expectantly. "Somethin' else, Jimbo...Somethin'...What was it, eh, boy?"

What else? His thoughts took him back to the woodlot again. Something with the chainsaw...

Think, man...Think!

He became aware of his hand again, it was shaking slightly as it rested on the top of the oil can. He pressed his hand down harder, gripping the handle, his pale blue eyes scanning the wall above the bench. So many wooden-handled tools, stained by the men who had used them, many of which had belonged to his father's father; smooth handles that contained the sweat of his family, generations of men who had toiled on the land.

A smile flickered across his craggy, sun-dried face. There she was again, as he'd always remember her. Their black and white wedding photograph, July 18th 1959, taken outside All Saints Anglican Church in Bayswater. The happiest day of his life.

He picked up the small framed picture, blew the dust away, then sat down on a paint-splattered wooden chair beside the tractor. The dog moved closer to him.

A swift flew into the barn like an arrow, darting and weaving its way into the rafters, chattering loudly upon reaching its nest. Jimbo raised his head, alert as always. The old man never batted an eye. He was thinking about his wife.

For a moment there she was again, standing in the barn doorway, a summer breeze pushing that green polka dot dress against her body. She looked about 30...young again...The light often played tricks, especially up here in the barn...Valerie had been gone these past ten years...

"She's not real, Jimbo...Just another beautiful mirage. Not real...a ghost..."

His bottom lip quivered. The dog placed its head on the old man's lap, looking up at him with warmth and concern. He scratched the dog's ears. "It's alright, boy, alright..."

He took a clean rag from his coveralls and dabbed his eyes, then he blew his nose.

The swift was making a racket with its mate, chattering loudly. It darted from the nest and flew low over the tractor and back into the sunlight.

The old man got up. He'd been sitting for over half an hour. Clearing his throat, he shuffled back to the work bench and picked up the oil. Then he reached for a small rounded file from a greasy wooden tray that held similar implements. He needed to sharpen the chain with the file.

Glancing at the dog, he put the file in his pocket next to a chewed stub of a pencil. "Remembered," he said. He patted his pocket whilst looking at the photograph of his wife.

The dog wagged its tail as it followed the old man out of the barn and back down the track to the woodlot. The old man started to sing a hymn, "All Things Bright and Beautiful", in his thin reedy tenor voice. He stopped abruptly.

It was then that he remembered that he'd forgotten to go to choir practice that morning.

Daniel Lillford

4: The box

If you can't say anything nice about someone…think it. And they did. In spades.

"That ole' bastard'll rot in hell come the day," Bing Westhaver thought as he passed Art Publicover going into Hubbards.

Normally two drivers who knew each other would each acknowledge the other with a friendly wave, the hand just off the wheel: the local road etiquette. Some would even honk, but those drivers tended to be younger and generally noisier.

Art Publicover couldn't give a rat's ass if Bing Westhaver, or any other half-witted South Shore sonofabitch, didn't wave. As far as he was concerned, most of humanity didn't amount to more than a pile of manure. Art didn't like people. He didn't like animals either, especially dogs. Dogs always made him uneasy.

Selma Dorey, who had known Art from the time she used to babysit the Publicover youngsters, recalled, "A no-good brat always gettin' into trouble, in an' outta school. Never proved, but everyone knows he burnt the old Morash fish shack down. Couldn't have been older than nine. Yup. An arsehole he was then, an arsehole he always would be…Can't change a bad seed…Yup."

Iona McRae chimed in with, "Least Wilma left him high an' dry, an' not befores time, in my opinion…"

"Mine neither; the stoopid woman," Selma said as she gently kicked her Tabby out from under the chair.

She picked the cat up and put it outside as she continued, "Used to beat her, knows that f'sure. Times I seen her with the black eyes, bruised face…Yup, down at the store, wearin' them shades in winter like nobody knows what's goin' on at home. Lord dyin' Jeezus…Yup."

Iona nodded solemnly as Selma took out another cigarette and lit it up with the dying embers from the previous one she was about to butt out, talking between puffs. "Youse remember when Cyril Cleveland confronted him an' got all his teef knocked out with a bat for his troubles?"

"I do."

"Yup...Got the dentures after that...Poor Cyril." Iona nodded grimly, then added, "But I think Cyril'd taken care'a Art if he weren't in no wheelchair...Man needs his legs in a fight, eh."

Selma grunted as she poured some rum into two tin cups. "Ah, Cyril Cleveland was always as useless as a sack full'a hammers. Besides, man had no business messin' in udders' affairs, right or wrong. Should'a stayed clear, left 'em to sort out their own marriage troubles. Them's the rules. Cyril know'd that."

"Well of course he did, Selma. He jest wanted to stand up for Wilma, that's all."

"In a wheelchair? Fat lotta good that did him, the great eejit."

"Anyway, man won out in the end, so there youse be. But even youse Selma, even youse, youse'd liked to have seen Art Publicover get his comeuppance, eh? No denyin' that. Knows I would, jest t'see his lyin' grin rejigged on the udder side of his face...All the same, we shouldn't speak ill'a the dead. Don't need bad luck brung on the home."

Selma nodded. She took a sip of rum from her tin cup, picked up the deck of well-thumbed playing cards, and started to shuffle them. Cigarette ash fell on her stained pinafore apron as she talked.

"Fancy hittin' poor Cleveland with a baseball bat whilst he's sittin' in his wheelchair," Iona said. "Talk 'bout a sittin' duck."

Selma Dorey chuckled wickedly to herself as she dealt out the cards. "Funeral tomorrow. It'll be a quiet one."

~

Wilma Publicover, Art's AWOL wife, was, before she became Mrs Publicover, Wilma Gertrude Himmelman from down East Chester way. At five feet 11 inches she was tall for a woman, taller than a helluva lot of men. She had a fine figure, willowy, long, slender legs, shoulder-length strawberry blonde hair, large breasts and a small waist.

Morton Hamm always said Wilma Himmelman had a butter-face. Everything about her was wonderful…but-her-face.

In her youth, Wilma had elicited her fair share of wolf-whistles as she passed building sites and from teens curb-crawling in their muscle cars. It never bothered her like it offended so many women. However, whenever she'd turned to see who had whistled, usually smiling, there was always a strange, Biblical response to her lopsided, buck-tooth grin and bottle-cap glasses. She wondered why men would say, "Jeezus H… Dear Lord in Heaven… Oh, Christ." And once she heard a roofer moan, "Holy shit! What a cryin' shame!"

She never understood why. Wilma was brought up to believe she was beautiful and that men would adore her. But they didn't. Mostly she'd been used and discarded. Her father had told her that men would cherish her, that the right man would worship the very ground she walked upon. And somewhere inside she still quietly believed that. Still hoped for it. Wilma had always been a simple, gentle soul. Some said, unkindly, that she was a bit thick.

Hans Himmelman loved his daughter very much and would have done everything within his power to stop his only child getting mixed up with Art Publcover, a known philanderer and no Lutheran. But he died prematurely in a road accident near the Tantallon turn-off on the 103. The police said that alcohol was a factor.

Hans had run the hardware store in Chester for nearly 25 years, having taken over from his father Otto, in 1972. He was well known and well liked. At the little church, his funeral was packed to overflowing.

"Sardines in dark suits," Earle Levy was overheard saying before his wife Thelma, elbowed him in the ribs.

After her father died, Wilma took over the store, more out of respect for his memory than finding her true vocation. She stuck it out for a few years before Morton Hamm made her an offer on the business and she accepted.

In hindsight, it was a paltry sum for a thriving business, but then Morty, as he was known to his friends in the Conservative Party, was as tight as the crab's ass and a very shrewd businessman. Those that knew Morty well always joked, "Morty always brung his bacon home!"

Others, who were less friendly and not of his political stripe, called the man a greedy pig behind his back.

~

But as much as Morton Hamm might or might not be a pig, he was not even in the same league as Art Publicover.

Wilma Himmelman was 31 years old when Art started making his advances known. He bought her flowers and chocolates. He took her to the movies. He was attentive, thoughtful, caring. He was the one. Or so she thought.

One night, when they were making out in his truck at the East River drive-in, he popped the question. No man had ever kissed her down there before, Wilma thought he was unique. She accepted.

They say that a year after Art was born, his mother, Hazel, turned to her husband, Ben, and said, "Out'a all our young'uns this one's got the cat's eyes. The cold ones."

Ben laughed. He didn't believe his wife was serious. But Hazel wasn't joking. She saw something in the toddler that disturbed her, made her uneasy. Art and his mother would never be close.

Young Art learned to fight early on. Having older brothers will do that. However, it was far from natural to try to drown one of your siblings in the bathtub. Katie and Tom, the twins, rescued Caspar; and if they hadn't been there that day, seven-year-old Art would most likely have killed nine-year-old Caspar. As it was, Art still managed to punch both Katie and Tom before they finally wrested his hands from Caspar's throat.

When his father gave him the belt, 12 lashes across the buttocks, the child hummed his way through the ordeal to a Hank Snow song. He never shed a tear.

Daniel Lillford

Ben thought Art was tough, if unusual, and he admired, albeit silently, the stubbornness of his littlest child. Hazel had other thoughts. She knew something perhaps only mothers can know about their offspring, and she felt it in her bosom that there was just something plain mean and wicked about Art. Something unhinged.

A few years after Ben died, Hazel found out how mean her youngest son could be. He had her moved, against her better judgment, into an old folks' home up near Blockhouse, the cheapest, most out-of-the-way place he could find.

Hazel was 77 years old, in reasonable health, no signs of dementia. Not that it mattered. Last year's fall on the ice, the suspected concussion, were all Art needed. Man had to work, he couldn't spend all his days looking after her; worrying about her. She was a drain on him.

He knew his siblings would come round to his way of thinking in time. Caspar was serving his country in the Balkans, so he was well out of the picture. This pleased and relieved Art. Tom and Katie had gone West years before, they both had good jobs in Calgary and growing families of their own.

Art was left to his own devices in caring for his mother, a woman whom he had never been fond of. Never loved. Now he barely tolerated her as he orchestrated her life through his tapestry of deceit.

It wasn't too long before he had bundled Hazel into the retirement home and brow-beaten her into selling the family home. Hazel had no fight left in her. Since his father had died, Art had watched the light in his mother's eyes grow dim. It was barely a pilot flame now.

He'd masterfully strung his siblings along, playing on the geographic distance, their obvious guilt and anything else that he could use as a psychological wedge to further his plans. Art was good at lying, always had been. A natural.

He'd told them the realty market was down and prices weren't so good. The house was old and in need of repair, a new roof for starters, so what did they expect? And if they didn't like the way he was handling things, they could all come back East and do it themselves, it was all the same to him. He'd be glad to wash his hands of the responsibility. They had it easy, he was the one doing all the running around. He was the one "looking after their mother". His point was hollow but effective.

In the end Art had read his siblings well. Only Caspar had kicked a little, but he was quite powerless to really challenge anything from so far away. He had a war to fight.

Art sent cheques for $15,000 to each of them and pocketed $40,000 for himself. And he never sold the woodlot, though he'd told them that he had. That land was worth another $12,000 at least.

Hazel died from a brain hemorrhage two months after her admittance. She was sad and alone. The last visitor she had seen was Art, the day he'd helped move her in. He never bothered to call to find out how his mother was doing. He didn't care.

To put the cherry on the cake, Caspar, Hazel's favourite son, was due on leave to visit her later that month. He attended his mother's funeral instead.

It was a tawdry affair. Art had really outdone himself this time. Six days earlier he'd been working in his shed, staining his mother's cheap pine coffin a muddy mahogany colour. The stain was a mixture of turpentine and some old boat paint. He didn't even wait for it to dry properly before he slapped on a coat of decking urethane from another old can he found on the shelf. By his calculations he'd saved well over $1,500 by doing it all himself.

The local hardware store supplied paltry brass handles, four at $3.50 a pop, for the pall bearers to grip as they carried Hazel from the church to the grave, where she was laid to rest beside her husband Ben. She almost ended up laid out on the church steps when two of the handles broke.

Frank Levy, one of the pall bearers, is still trying to find a dry-cleaner who can get the urethane stains out of the only dark suit he's ever owned.

Tom and Katie were too bereaved, ashamed and guilt-ridden to notice their brother's parsimony; but Caspar, noticed.

In full military uniform of a sergeant-major, service medals gleaming, Caspar looked proud, every bit a soldier, straight as a rod and always the handsome boy in the Publicover family. At the end of the funeral he strode up to Art and grabbed him by the throat, drawing his little brother eyeball to eyeball.

Before he was restrained and the two pulled apart, Caspar said to Art through gritted teeth, "You're no brother a'mine, you cheap, low-down sonofabitch!"

Art retorted, "Oh, that's a fine thing to be sayin' at our mudder's funeral!"

Caspar had to be held fast because he wanted to commit an Old Testament act on his youngest brother. They never spoke to each other again.

Only one brother would ever feel ashamed of his actions that day.

~

After ten years of marriage and ten years of emotional and physical abuse, Wilma decided she'd finally had enough. Her 41st birthday had come and gone. She glanced at the subscription to The National Geographic, Art's so-called gift, and held back a muffled grunt that lingered in her chest like phlegm from a bronchial infection. Every gift he'd ever bought her was for himself.

It was the morning after her birthday, September 17th. Her suitcases were packed.

As she waited for the taxi, she drank her coffee in the kitchen, looking around one last time over the things she had done to try to make this house a home. Her geraniums climbed against the window, the largest nearly three feet tall. The curtains she'd sewn to size, the little ribbons to tie them mid-way. All the painting and scrubbing, the time...My God, the time...Ten years of marriage... Three miscarriages.

She was glad she didn't have a child, his child. But in her saddest moments she would still curl up in a ball on the bed in the middle of the day and weep with a dreadful feeling of loss. It was a loss she could never articulate without sounding self-pitying.

Her once golden hair was almost silver now. She took her features in the small mirror that hung above the "Greek's Meats" calendar near the kitchen door. Her lips were thin. She took off her thick glasses; her cobalt eyes now looked sunken and numbed. Her skin was sallow, lined before its time. She hardly recognized herself.

The clock gently ticked as 7 am drew closer. Light shone across the pine kitchen table from a window near the range. The breadboard had remnants of cheese, crumbs and egg where Art had made his sandwiches earlier. The bread knife would be covered in margarine: he never bothered to get a butter knife from the drawer, never cleaned up after himself, never had. Ten years of marriage...

She looked out the window toward the woods. The leaves on the poplar trees were already starting to turn. She could hear a chainsaw humming in the distance. *That's where he'll be*, she thought, *at the woodlot*.

The taxi arrived and honked.

Wilma picked up her suitcases, the very same ones she'd used on her honeymoon. Pale blue imitation leather with white piping.

The honeymoon had been a damp and cheerless affair in Parrsboro. It rained the five whole days they were there.

Things had changed between them then. She never understood why. Art, when he wasn't in the local tavern, was in the motel watching television, a six-pack of beer by his side and packets of Players cigarettes for company.

It was on the third night of their marriage that he first hit her. She blocked his view of the hockey game for a moment, and in that moment the Leafs scored.

She cried herself to sleep whilst he continued to watch Hockey Night in Canada. He never apologized, never tried to comfort her. He said nothing, just drank and smoked and watched television.

Later, when he entered her as she pretended to be asleep, it was as if an animal was mounting her. There was nothing caring or loving about it, it was a purely functional act...Ten years of marriage...

Daniel Lillford

She left a lipstick-stained coffee cup on the sink, hardly thinkable a few days ago, opened the door and walked away.

When Wilma arrived at the Halifax airport she met Cyril Cleveland waiting in his wheelchair underneath the American Airlines sign, where he had said he'd be. Cyril looked like a naughty schoolboy, except he was as bald as an old tire and his greying beard reached his pot belly, making him look like a roadie with ZZ Top. The "Things Go Better With Cocaine" t-shirt under his leather vest isn't going to make it any easier when dealing with the customs officials, she thought. They'd most likely strip his wheelchair looking for contraband. They did that in Los Angeles, so he'd told her.

She smiled at him, and he smiled at her, they clutched at each other's hands, almost childishly.

The next day they were living in his hideaway on the Mexican coast.

Art told anyone who wanted to listen that he'd kicked Wilma out. "Good riddance!," he'd joked with a bitter twist to his mouth.

Morton Hamm knew instinctively that Art was full of it. His years of Conservative political shenanigans had briefed him well in spotting liars. As he said, "When you belong to the liars' club, we're a pretty hard bunch to fool."

Morton had always liked Wilma. Okay, she may have had lefty liberal leanings, she was a bit dim, but still, no woman deserved the likes of Art Publicover. He genuinely hoped she'd be happy in Mexico. Though he did wonder what she saw in Cyril Cleveland, a known pot-smoker with socialist views, a man who subscribed to The Guardian Weekly and had a picture of Lenin on his bedroom wall! It was actually a picture of John Lennon, not that Morton would've known the difference.

"An' the guy has no hair, been as bald as a coot since he was twenty!," he told Muriel McLeod as she paid for her bag of roofing nails and a picture frame. Not that Muriel cared, but Mort continued, "Must be true what they say 'bout bald guys, eh?," and he winked at her in triplicate. Muriel wondered if Morton wasn't developing a nervous tic.

Wilma had had few friends who would pay her a call, and those who did come around always timed their arrival and departure for when Art was not there. Now that she had left him, there was no reason for anyone to call. And nobody did.

That suited Art just fine.

When Wilma had been gone for almost eighteen months, Stanley Backman dropped in on Art because he'd heard, from Morton, that Art was thinking about selling his wood-splitter. Stanley called out from his truck but received no reply. Art's Ford Ranger was parked in the drive, so the man couldn't be too far away, or so Stanley thought.

He got out of his truck and ambled up to the porch, called out Art's name again and waited. Still nothing. He opened the screen door and looked inside.

It was the smell that hit him first.

He called out again, still nothing. He sat himself down on a kitchen chair near the front door and waited, running his spidery fingers through his close-cropped white hair. He took out his makings and rolled himself a Drum cigarette, taking a long look around as he drew in the smoke.

It was a horrible sight. Dust covered every surface. The window curtains were drawn and faded. Flies buzzed around an overloaded kitchen trash can. Empty baked beans tins were everywhere, some resting against the cupboard doors and baseboards. Boxes of Olands beer were piled up all over the place, the stale smell of empties stagnating the atmosphere.

Wilma's once-proud geraniums were twisted, dead wrecks in parched pots. The linoleum floor was grease-stained and scuffed from heavy work boots, it looked as if it hadn't ever been mopped. The range was covered with blackened pots and pans. A wall on one side showed signs of having caught on fire. The light switch was paw marked with oil stains; one clear thumbprint was visible.

The filth aside, what struck Stanley the most was the feeling in the house, the smell, and it wasn't the mould he'd caught a whiff of when he walked in. No, there was something else here… Something dead, or dying. It made him uneasy. As he looked around he felt the urge to explore further, but his common decency wouldn't allow that.

He finished up his cigarette then got up to leave. His braces got caught on a nail sticking out of the chair, which he upended without meaning to.

As he picked up the chair, a large grey rat shot past the range and skittered off toward darker corners inside the house.

"Lord almighty..." Stanley Backman muttered.

He didn't wait for Art to show, he was feeling dirty, as if lice had started to crawl down his neck.

He got to his truck, sat and waited, thought about Del, his wife, who always kept their house so neat and tidy, and how Del had always said that Wilma put her to shame because the Publicover house was so clean you could eat your supper off the bathroom tiles. Stanley shook his head. He was glad he hadn't looked in the bathroom.

He thought of Wilma now, remembering her sitting reading on the porch, or tending her flowers. He always thought she had the saddest smile he'd ever seen.

Stanley turned the key, put his Bronco into gear and reversed slowly out of the yard. He decided he wouldn't tell Del about what he had seen. There was enough gossip in the world.

He drove home. Said a prayer for Wilma, asking God to look after her.

Art had watched Stanley pull out of his drive from the safety of the garden shed. Stanley was well liked in the community, respected, and Art despised him for it; and there wasn't a snowflake's chance in hell he'd ever sell his wood splitter to Mr. Morally Upstanding, Churchgoing, Pillar of the Community, Stanley fucking Backman. Besides, he didn't need Backman's money, not through any legal exchange.

Art made sure that Stanley was well gone before he turned his attention back to what he had been doing before he was interrupted. He moved from the cobwebbed window toward the open floorboards he'd hastily covered up with an apple crate when he heard the Bronco coming down his drive. He shoved the crate out of the way and reached down into the floor, bringing up a rusty, battered old cash box.

A wicked grin turned up the corners of his thin mouth momentarily. Even in joy Art looked cruel.

One of Art's true pleasures in life was to peruse the death notices in the local paper. He got a genuine kick out of it. He nearly fell off his chair when he read in last Tuesday's *Chronicle-Herald* that Percy J. Harnish had died. He laughed, lit a cigarette, smiled quietly to himself, his eyes glazing over with the look of man deep in scheming thoughts.

He'd known Percy had been unwell, but he was a tough old bird, and tough old birds around these parts usually lived to be a hundred. So the news was such a pleasant surprise.

He calculated who he might have to deal with over the estate. Percy had outlived all his brothers and sisters. Art reckoned the old man must have been 96, not 86 as the paper reported. Those eejits were always getting facts wrong.

Anyway, it was perfect. He'd be dealing with the children or, better still, the grandchildren. And even better, they were less likely to know anything about him, and therefore less likely to ask any awkward questions.

Over the years Art had always been watchful of certain properties, houses that were of an original rock foundation, preferably without major structural renovations, at least 150 years old, and belonging to certain first families to the area. Percy J. Harnish's homestead fitted the bill to the letter.

Art's *modus operandi* was always the same, and it had served him well over the years. It was simple, dead simple.

Early on, when he knew that some relative was at the deceased's estate cleaning up, Art would turn up in his truck and invent a cock and bull story about the deceased having asked him to clear out the basement and out buildings some weeks before, but what with one thing and another, either being sick with flu, or just run off his feet, well here he was now...And after the relative explained to Art that the person had just died, Art would always act shocked, deeply saddened, sometimes even verging on tears, but only if he thought a performance was necessary. He only used the latter when he suspected he was being judged and knew he was dealing with a hardnose.

But no matter what, he'd always say, "I'm so sorry for your loss."

Then he would talk about the deceased like he or she was an old friend. Art by name, artful by nature.

He never laid it on thickly. Most of his knowledge came from the careful study of the obituary, plus local gossip he'd picked up over the years. Whatever his faults, Art listened better than most and, more importantly, he recalled detail; uncannily-minute detail.

To watch him work a mourning family member was to witness a perfect scoundrel in action. Art had been in the cartage and antique game for nearly 35 years. He'd tried his hand at most everything at one time or another, but in this world he'd found a place and he'd flourished. The barn was stuffed to the rafters with fishing and farming antiques from "clearing out" basements and barns throughout Lunenburg County. There was a mound of glass buoys, which he could sell to the city dealers for $20 a pop, knowing they'd sting their punters for $40, if not more, depending on the colour of the glass. He kept the big glass buoys for himself. He knew he could get upwards of $400 for just one of them.

All tax free. What the government didn't know...

Mostly he sold his best finds to dealers in Montreal and Toronto, and got rid of the common, the modern, in the occasional yard sale, though he didn't like yard sales one little bit. Being nice to day-trippers looking for deals was like dealing with a boil rubbing against his collar. Chit-chat with amateur vultures had always annoyed him.

In 35 years he had not found what he had always known was out there, somewhere...That was, until yesterday.

Art held the bundles of cash in his hands. There were thousands. Rolls of $50 bills, $20 bills, all the smaller denominations. Aged rubber bands that crumbled to the touch, but the bills stayed rolled tight. Art had guessed there was probably $30,000; but on final count, which he was engaged in before Stanley Backman showed up, he'd gone past $52,000 and still hadn't touched the smaller bills.

"God love youse, Percy! God love youse, you tight-fisted son-of-a-whore!"

He chuckled to himself, barely containing his glee, and half-wished Percy J. Harnish could see him. "That'd piss the old slut-rock right up the fucking wall!"

He'd found the battered cash box hidden in the rock basement wall near the furnace chimney. Art used a wet straw broom to sweep away the spider's homes, making sure the wall was dampened down. He then strafed the wall with his raven eyes, looking for cracks that seemed unusual or holes that appeared unnatural to the structure.

It was an uneven rock two feet from the dirt floor that caught his attention. There was an exposed lip around two sides, just enough for fingers to dislodge it with a bit of elbow grease.

After a small struggle, Art was holding a loose granite block in his hands. He nearly soiled his pants with anticipation. The excitement made him tingle all over, his breathing became heavy and short, but there was no stopping him now.

He shone the flashlight into the wall, and there was his prize: the late Percy J. Harnish's hidden safety deposit box, now divested of its secrecy.

Here was what he had always wished to find: the black-market gold, the undeclared taxable income, the Rainy Day Fund, the old Prohibition spondulicks.

As a child Art had heard about the older fellas hiding their hard-earned away like squirrels hide acorns in middens. The Great Depression had made many of the local fishermen fearful of the banks.

Then there were the rum runners, estates that had been bought and maintained through the proceeds of criminal activity, fortunes made and hidden during the Prohibition decade. Money and booze were hidden everywhere back in those days. As Earle Levy would quote his grandfather, a known rum runner and a contemporary of Percy J. Harnish, "There was so much money 'bout, they even had it comin' outta the cat's arse!"

Art had come across his fair share of Prohibition liquor. Aged whisky was still aged whisky and well worth the price to a collector. One fella in Montreal bought from him a half-crate of Balvenie single malt, circa 1927, for nearly $5,000. That was back in 1983. Crime was still paying.

~

Earlier that morning Miranda Campbell, Percy's only granddaughter, who had no interest in her grandfather's house nor its contents, had been relieved when Art Publicover showed up out of the blue to take care of a "verbal contract" he had with the late Mr. Harnish. She had no earthly reason not to trust what Art told her, and he appeared honestly stunned and upset when she told him about the old man's passing. He seemed to know a lot about her grandfather, more than she did, so she naturally assumed they were friends, good neighbours.

Miranda was a city girl, she had no fondness for the country, so the sooner she was out of "bugsville" the better.

Art Publicover couldn't have timed his run better. He smiled like a barracuda when Miranda asked him if he wouldn't mind looking over the contents of the main house and giving her a price, this on top of the contents in the outbuildings and sheds.

"Of course it's no problem, my dear... But, jeez, I can't see as I can afford to give youse much for all that heavy old furniture. Maybes you'd be better off talkin' to that junk collector fella in Hubbards, on the main street, eh? Youse know the one, fella from Toronto."

Art was talking about his only rival in the district for miles, John Mellor, a man Art truly detested for no other reason than that John Mellor didn't come from around here, therefore he was by implication, a foreigner. And nobody trusts come-from-aways. Not around here.

Miranda didn't know John Mellor, but she did think that Art was being an honest man in giving her a choice.

Then Art added, before Miranda could reach a decision, "Course, personally speakin', I wouldn't deal with him. But that's jest me, up to youse, my dear, it's your stuff. Wouldn't want a nice young woman such as yourself gettin' the wool pulled by no come-from-aways, if youse know what I mean."

He'd set the prejudice in motion knowing all too well the deep rooted tribalism of the county. "Mellor's not a fair man to deal with?" she said.

Art scratched his right ear, squinted and looked like a wizened gnome, then said in a sheepish tone, "I can't speak ill'a no man, my dear. Besides that, we're in the same game, youse might say, him an' me. Same business. So I can't feather me own nest without lookin' bad, eh? Havin' what them smart fellas, what they call 'exterior' motives, eh?"

Miranda laughed at him, his silly malapropism, but she liked him, found him endearing in an impish sort of way.

Art laughed, too...at her, because he knew he'd got her played out like a trout, and he thought as he laughed, *That's it, youse fat-arsed city bitch, youse jest keep thinkin' you're dealin' with the village eejit...that's it, ha, ha, ha!*

As he took in the heavy, 1930s, walnut dining table and chairs, the original Tancook hooked rugs and the art-deco lamps and fittings, Art calculated a profit of at least $12,000 in this room alone. He fidgeted and squinted, then, with a heavy sigh as if he was doing her a favour, he offered Miranda Campbell a grand for the lot, and he wasn't charging for removal costs.

She looked around, uncertain. She'd been hoping for a few thousand dollars.

Art read the moment. "Course, if youse want t'git a second opinion… All right, I'm a softy, I knows it. Pretty girl smiles, I go all weak-kneed."

Miranda positively beamed. Charmed. She hadn't been called a pretty girl for many years.

"Tell youse what, my dear. I'll give youse $1,500, an' I can't be no fairer than that, eh?"

She laughed, then said naively, "There's a lot more rooms, Mr. Publicover."

Art grunted, grinned, somewhat bemused, as he took in what

looked like an original Robert Norwood photograph hanging in the hallway. Could pick up $750, maybe more for that one.

"Well of course, my dear, of course! Jeez, one at a time, eh. I don't pick me spondulicks off the crab apple tree!"

She laughed at his turn of phrase and he watched her breasts heave with jollity, forgetting momentarily his business at hand. He followed her about like a purring cat from one room to another.

Not that he was too surprised, but it was one buckshee moment after another. Quite the day. Indeed, a beautiful day.

Miranda Campbell only annoyed him once. She wanted the Wedgewood dinner set, not because she knew what it was worth, but because she liked the pretty pattern.

Art smiled, gritted his teeth. He liked the pretty pattern too. That set was worth $2,000 to the right collector. "Ah, well, can't win 'em all..."

He waved as he watched Miranda drive away. By his rough calculations he'd made $40,000 already, and he hadn't even begun to explore. He smiled wickedly as Miranda's car disappeared from view. "God love stoopid fat-arsed whores."

Art had felt a tingle of excitement all through his body when he'd discovered Percy's treasure, but he couldn't understand why his left arm was still tingling and his breath seemed short. He put these symptoms down to feeling elated, the happiest he could ever remember, and he thought he should get some food into him. That must be why he felt light-headed, nothing more. A can of baked beans would do the trick.

If he'd had a mirror to look into, he mightn't have felt so good. He would have seen a slight bluish tinge to his lips and a greying of his skin.

But he wasn't thinking about his general health as he made his way across the puddle-ridden drive toward his house, the metal cash box in his hand containing over $58,000, give or take a buck.

Twenty feet from his porch he felt a terrible pain in his chest; it twisted him around and his left arm went dead. He dropped the cash box as he fell to his knees.

He tried to catch his breath, but the next attack hauled him over into the mud, where his paralyzed face could only stare at the box lying in a muddy puddle beside his Ford's front driver's wheel. He wanted to reach for it but found he couldn't move at all.

Nothing was moving, every muscle seemed to have packed up, and yet here he was, still breathing.

He wanted to curse, but found no voice; not a sound came out. He was like a slug that had just hit a pinch of salt. He felt like his body was dissolving into the damp earth and there was nothing he could do about it.

As dusk flooded into the daylight, Art began to think. It was all he could do.

He thought about Wilma for the first time in more than a year. He wished she was here now. Then he wished that he hadn't wished that at all. He wouldn't want her to see him like this.

He wished Stanley Backman would come back.

He thought about his siblings. He remembered his father, Ben. For a moment he felt very sad, very alone. He didn't like the feeling at all. He never liked feeling weak, vulnerable; that was for all those chinless bastards and whores out there, it wasn't for Art Publicover.

He heard the phone inside the house ring five times, then the caller hung up, which meant it was probably a local call. Might've been Percy's granddaughter. She had nice tits. He never had invested in an answering machine. This annoyed him now.

The night brought its own terror. Mosquitoes feasted on his limp carcass. One landed on his eyelid and all he could do was acknowledge it, knowing it was filling itself with his blood.

A raccoon moved out from the pine trees on the edge of the property. It scuttled forward, then stopped, cocking its head. Art thought it was grinning at him.

The raccoon then sniffed the air, quickened its pace and made for the underneath of the house. Something had spooked it.

The wind picked up and Art could hear thunder coming in off the Atlantic. Weather report had said it was going to rain tonight. He wondered if he would feel the rain when it came.

Along with his eyesight, his hearing was fine…But he wished he was deaf and blind when he heard them coming.

Stanley Backman did come back, two days later. What he found made him throw-up his breakfast.

Wild dogs, possibly coyotes, had dragged the body of Art Publicover every which way. They had eaten their fill and the crows were still picking at theirs when Stanley pulled into the drive.

At first glance, Stanley thought Art must have shot some animal in his yard and left it there, which he wouldn't put past the man. It was the oily stained "John Deere" ball cap still resting on the bloodied, eyeless head that made Stanley utter, "Oh, sweet Jeezus…"

Then he had puked.

The Coroner's finding was that Art Publicover had suffered a series of strokes, paralyzing him, and had been attacked and eaten whilst he was still alive. It had not been a quick death.

After the funeral, Wilma stood in the front yard of her old house with Stanley Backman. She was dressed in a powder-grey, pin-striped suit with a black turtle-neck sweater. The green rubber boots she'd borrowed from Del didn't match her outfit, but were appropriate for the surroundings.

She couldn't believe the state the house was in, or so she said. But she knew she'd been married for ten long years to a pig of a man. A callous and a heartless man. Still, nobody deserves to die like he did.

Nobody.

Life was good in Mexico with Cyril, and she didn't need this millstone of a memory around her neck. Not now, not ever. This house held nothing but wasted years and a sadness she wasn't sure she'd ever truly shake off.

They stood near Art's Ford Ranger, puddles all around them. Some yellow police tape still flicked across the porch railing, gingerly moving in a ghost breeze.

"Don't know exactly what to do with it all, Stan… Just don't know."

She sighed and gently shook her head. Stanley nodded, glanced at her tanned face, her silver hair in a ponytail. She'd let it grow, long like it used to be when she was younger. Wilma looked good, healthy. Best he'd seen her in years. She wasn't wearing those thick glasses anymore. He wondered if she hadn't had some dental work done. Her smile was...Her face seemed different somehow.

"Lotta money tied up in the barn, all them collectibles he stored away. Whole place is bursting at the seams. Could get John Mellor to look it over. Sure he'll give youse a good deal. He's a fair man."

She nodded, tried to smile. "It's the house, Stan. Be just as well to burn it to the ground, be done with it. Not fit to live in anymore, 'cept for rodents."

Her rubber boot kicked a half-submerged metal box sideways. "Goddamn junk everywhere...I don't know what to do."

Stanley picked up the cash box. "Be glad to help youse out, Wilma. Me an' Del, wouldn't be no trouble."

He put the rusty cash box in the back of the Ford, where it rested beside an art-deco lamp stand and some tools. He never gave it a second thought.

Wilma said nothing for a minute. She just stared at the place where Art had died. It didn't seem real. But she wasn't sad, not for him.

"D'you think he'd have minded, Stan?"

"What's that?"

"Oh, you know, nobody there, not a soul... at his funeral?"

Stanley rolled himself a cigarette. Then he almost said something he'd wanted to say for over 30 years: No offence, Wilma, but your husband was the meanest, cheapest, lowest asshole I've ever know'd in me whole goddamn life. Why in hell would anybody bother comin' to his funeral? Aloud he said, "You were there...Art was lucky."

Wilma looked at Stanley, nodded her head gently, thought on the word "duty," then walked a little toward the porch, looking at the remnants of the police tape. "Think they'll get those wild dogs?"

Stanley shrugged, blew some smoke into the overcast day, ran his fingers over the Ford's hood. "I'll buy the truck from youse, and the wood splitter."

Daniel Lillford

5: The light in the dunes

The click-clacking of his wife's knitting needles brought Charles' eyes back to the hearth; to Josette, with her wicker basket of wool, her hands moving dexterously, like the second hand on a clock or a well-oiled piston. Her lined face concentrated on the task at hand, sleeves for Noel's blue birthday cardigan. The boy would be 14 in a month. The kitchen smelled of stew, some of which still simmered in the cast iron pot hanging on the chimney crane off to one side of the fireplace.

The grandfather clock in the hallway struck the hour. Charles Dubois glanced at his fob watch, corrected the time, wound it, then popped it back into his grey waistcoat.

Under the lamplight at the kitchen table, still poring over her homework, their eldest daughter, Marie-Louise, was nibbling the end of a pencil, deep in thought.

As Charles stood up, the paper he'd been reading fell from his lap onto the floor, disturbing the sleeping cat. He placed a gentle hand on Marie-Louise's shoulder. The girl looked up and smiled at her father, squeezing his hand. He was glad his daughter was still awake; she being in the room would curtail any arguments before bedtime.

Kneeling, he put a shovelful of coal on the fire. His wife pulled her legs together and away from him.

Moving to the window, he looked through a crack in the black-out curtain, wondering if she would ever forgive him.

"The patrol is late tonight," he said.

Josette ignored him. Her needles kept up their metallic rhythm as the coal hissed and the wind whistled down the chimney.

"Not like them," Charles said. "No. Not like them at all."

He moved out of the kitchen and into the hallway, taking his old pea-coat off a peg whilst shoving his feet into his work boots. The cat came to find him, sitting close to his threadbare tartan slippers, watching, blinking. It made a strange yowling sound and stared at him oddly, its big yellow eyes searching. He smiled at the cat, rubbed its head, turned for the door, reached for his battered trilby.

"If they catch you, what good will you be to us in a German prison? Or shot?"

He held the door handle, stopped short by his wife's bitter tone. "I'm going to check on the cows, that's all."

He didn't wait for Josette to respond; he was outside in an instant. Had he waited, he would have heard, "Yes, well you're a good one for the cows. All the pretty cows."

Marie-Louise gave her mother a pained look as the front door slammed shut.

A storm had been brewing all day. That afternoon Charles had watched the sky darkening over the English Channel and felt the wind freshen. All the signs were in play that they were going to be in for it tonight.

The hated curfew was in effect, so he knew he had to be careful walking about of an evening, even around his own farm. One didn't argue with the Germans and their rules. They could be right bastards.

What moon there was showed enough of the sea to behold a boiling mass of whitecaps.

As he moved toward the cow shed, he looked up the road, a wide, meandering gravel track between the dunes and the seawall. The wind was picking up, a shrill-like whistling that rose and fell without harmony.

He heard their guttural voices before he saw the German patrol. From the safety of the cow shed he watched four soldiers, rifles slung over their shoulders, doing what they always did at this time of night since they had occupied the island. They were in good spirits by the sound of it. There was laughter.

A light suddenly shone on the farmhouse. Charles saw a young soldier, perhaps no more than 19, looking upward toward the bedroom windows. He lingered as his comrades moved further along the road. The burly sergeant called out and the young soldier turned the torchlight off, rejoining his squad at a trot.

Someone said something. More laughter.

Charles waited until the patrol was no longer visible before he walked across the road and made his way through the dunes and down the slipway to the beach. The tide was on the turn; breakers were already pounding into the shoreline with a deafening ferocity. The wind pinned his cheekbones back.

He took off his hat and leaned his body into the wall, the cool granite soothing his troubled head... Peace. No arguments, no animosity or bitterness, no snide accusations, no silent hatred. Just this...Peace... and quiet, too; yes, even here when the sea is raging with Poseidon's wrath. He slid down the wall and rested on his haunches.

Thunder grumbled, lightning bolts struck out like so many neon veins into the blackness. It seemed to him that he had watched this prelude many times before. He smiled at nature's constancy. Storms had always made him feel that much more alive...

She had said that; that his eyes shone when the weather got rough. She noticed things about him, the little things that Josette never mentioned, or hadn't ever noticed. Or didn't care about.

He thought about Katherine now, her dark green eyes, long fingers, a laugh that...He could still hear her laughter after all these long months. It was like an echo he'd kept hidden away; his own precious secret. That at least was still his.

He wished she was close again, as she had been all through that last month, when they lived every clandestine moment fully, both knowing it would not last. That beautiful month of May, before the bloody war came to the island, before she had to leave...

He'd been such a fool. A reckless fool. Very few secrets are ever kept hidden on a small island. There are too many eyes. Too many tongues. Besides, any woman with half a nose will always smell another woman on her man, even if she hasn't loved that man or slept with him for years.

Not that it matters. The aftermath is so ludicrously territorial and predictable. Wounded pride and misplaced vanity. The hollow moral point. And there's no forgiveness. Just God and children.

He closed his eyes. He loved his children, and he had loved Josette, once. Was that so long ago? Yes, a lifetime ago. Now he just felt old; so middle aged, so dreadfully unhappy.

Breakers were pounding into the German's steel tank traps laid out upon the beach like hundreds of twisted crowns of thorns. To his right, further up the coast, Russian prisoners of war had built a network of bunkers. It was common knowledge that the Germans used the Russians as slave labour and treated them cruelly. Rumour had it that if a Russian died on the job, the Germans just cemented his remains into the walls of the fortifications.

Charles didn't doubt that. He'd witnessed German barbarism and knew what they were capable of. The Germans had managed to turn this beach's natural beauty to shit with their concrete bunkers, steel traps and barbed wire...their awful war.

He hadn't thought about his father for a very long while; but there he was again, telling his stories, always seriously, when the nights were like this night, when the wind rattled the window panes and howled down the chimney, when they had sat together drinking hot chocolate by the hearth after his mother and three sisters had gone up to bed. The old man would light his pipe and after a few puffs, he'd tell his tales to his only son.

"T'weren't no farm, not in the strictest sense, though of course they farmed for appearances' sake. No, back in those times this house always served a darker purpose."

As a boy he'd often wondered at the incongruous, cemented-in, oblong crevices in parts of the granite walls around the farmhouse. His father had told him they were cuts gouged out of the stone for pointing muskets from within, and that you could still see the bevelled edges where a musket or a flintlock pistol could easily be moved left and right, up or down.

In the 18th century this was a wrecker's house. On nights like this one, when passing ships were out there in the channel, the wreckers would be on the beach with a lantern, trying to lure their victim onto the rocks, pretending to be a safe port in a storm. The bay was a ships' graveyard thanks to those devils. It was a dirty murderous business.

"Not Christian men, that's f'sure. You ever see the one they call 'the Captain', he's the one with the lamp, you run like hell itself was after you, and say your prayers as you go!"

Charles had heard many stories and myths about local ghosts and the fairy roads in the dunes. The man with the lamp was an old, old story, passed down from generation to generation, but it was also the only local story that had an unambiguous link to the farmhouse where he lived, where his family had lived for over 200 years. And it was more than a possibility that some of his own ancestors had been wreckers.

He'd asked his father if 'the Captain' was a ghost.

"Some say...Others say 'tis a demon, no less...All I know is, you ever see a strange light out in the dunes, you come home, boy, and be quick about it."

His father's earnest face stared back at him now. The man was not by nature a jocular fellow, never had been. His seriousness went hand in glove with the starkness with which he viewed the world around him; though he was not unkind and possessed an endless supply of patience.

Charles wished he could talk to his father now. But even if it were possible to summon up the dead, he knew what his old man would say, and that he'd most likely quote some passage out of the Bible for moral emphasis, and tell him that he'd made his bed, and so must he lie in it, if only for the sake of his children. Personal happiness never took precedence over duty, not in his father's world.

"Pride an' vanity, the devil's favourite cards," he'd said it often enough throughout the years.

The sound of gunfire shattered Charles' thoughts. Two distinct rapid rounds, then a third. Shouting, not too distant; movement, perhaps boots running. The voices of the German soldiers fought with the wind, but he knew it was the patrol coming back, and that they were in a hurry.

He moved slowly along the seawall and crouched low, finding the shadows, then up the slipway and into the dunes on his hands and knees.

He could see the soldiers moving back along the road in haste. Another gunshot echoed into the night.

Somewhere further down the coast, where the small garrison was barracked, the incremental whine of a hand-cranked siren went into action. A powerful searchlight opened on the beach, raking it backwards and forwards. The wash of the light suffused the area in a shifting pale blue aura.

Charles flattened himself out and watched through the marram grass as jackboots and field grey uniforms moved past him on the road. Their voices were anxious, they sounded scared.

One of the soldiers had been wounded, or so it seemed, and two of his comrades supported him. His body was limp, head on chest, boots dragging.

The wind was starting to howl now, a real gale erupting, and the sky opened with bolts of lightning across the bay, followed by a hard driving rain.

The unimpeded burly sergeant, rifle at the ready, was lit up for the briefest of moments. His eyes were wide, frightened, as he yelled at his men to hurry up, all the while keeping his gaze on where they had come from. The relentless rain only hastened their retreat down the road toward the barracks and the wailing siren.

Charles thought that perhaps the Germans had happened upon a commando raid; there had been a few of them in this area in the last six months. But it didn't seem right, not in these conditions. It would be too dangerous to land men here, crazy as the English might be.

In a few minutes the rain had thoroughly soaked him. His woollen clothes weighed heavy upon his slim frame. He got to his feet slowly and moved cautiously, staying in the shadows until he reached the road.

The patrol were out of sight now, though he still heard their voices carried in the wind. He made a beeline toward the farmhouse, looking forward to the warmth within and perhaps a second helping of rabbit stew to take the chill out of his bones.

Curious, he looked to where the Germans had run from.

The rain was sweeping in off the ocean now and visibility was not good, but there was no mistaking a distant light swaying left, then right, in a gentle arc about 300 yards from where he stood on the road. He thought it must be commandos; they must have landed...But commandos wouldn't use a light on a raid. He stared hard, trying to make some sense out of it.

The yellow light moved closer, brighter, mesmeric, almost as if it were hanging there in mid-air at times. He found himself frozen, hypnotized by it, peering into the pelting rain trying to make out what it was that was coming toward him. The light came onward, still swaying left, then right, then back again. Even in this filthy weather, Charles knew that what he was seeing was not of this time.

Unconsciously, he crossed himself.

A bolt of lightning struck into the dunes near the seawall, momentarily back-lighting the figure of a tall man dressed in a cape that flapped behind him like a flag. This figure now turned in the direction of the farmhouse. It seemed to rush onward, propelled momentarily, then draw back, linger, looking out toward the sea.

Charles could see that the man was wearing what looked like a fancy-dress costume; something straight out of those illustrations in Treasure Island, his favourite book when he was a boy. He was wearing a tricorn hat, a black frock coat with what looked like bright silver buttons, and knee-high riding boots.

As this figure glided ever closer, he appeared not to walk the earth at all, but float along hidden currents, or walk a pathway only he knew was there.

Charles felt his legs were like iron, as if the gravel road had gripped him fast. He tried to turn away, but the light held him spellbound.

The lantern kept swaying in its rhythmical motion, putting the face of the man who carried it into light and then into darkness. It was the face in the light that frightened Charles Dubois to his very marrow.

Instinctively, he started to pray: The Lord's Prayer came quickly, the words tumbling out of his mouth in a rush, striking the air, pleading for help. "—on earth as it is in heaven. Give us this day—"

The caped figure moved ever closer; a floating demonic creature, its liverish eyes and long, wolf-like features moved in and out of the shadows of the lamp, displaying the cruellest of smiles. Its cape now luffed upwards, giving the appearance of wings.

Charles wanted to sink into the road and hide, but his limbs would not obey. "—but deliver us from evil, for thine—"

His body felt so cold now, his teeth started to chatter out of control, like ice shaken in a tumbler, and the words of the prayer became a foreign babble of incoherence. And still he could not take his eyes from the swaying lamplight. His heart was beating like an off-kilter metronome, and his body felt like it was going to shake itself into oblivion.

The evil face of the spectre was almost upon him now, and the lamp started swinging in revolutions of its own accord, as if it were not attached to anything at all.

A kaleidoscope of swirling images assaulted Charles' senses. He saw an ancient ship in heavy weather breaking apart on the rocks, masts crashing down with sails and spars falling on those below, its deck splintering, the hull rolling in whitecaps, over and over toward the beach. Then murders committed on the sands and in the shallows; the clubbing of survivors with crude picks and shillelaghs. Cargo washing ashore, wooden boxes and casks swirling about, carried by breakers and driven onto the shoreline where the dark shadows of rough men retrieved the wreck's goods as the sea brought in the drowned and the almost dead with the pickings. He saw a wounded man spewing seawater, asking for help, for mercy, only to be bludgeoned to death where he lay by a tall man in a tricorn hat, carrying a lamp. This man turned to face Charles now, as if he himself were the very epicentre of all this carnage, all this wickedness. The man smiled. It was a grotesque smile.

Then everything became calm, gentle. Charles saw his father sitting in his boat, mending a crab pot, and there he was as a boy, helping him.

Daniel Lillford

He saw a younger Josette, smiling, picking daffodils down by the marsh, as he remembered her when they were courting; and there were his three children when they were small, happily playing in the dunes, laughing, running after each other...

Laughter...her laughter. He saw her green eyes staring back at him with so much warmth and tenderness; so close he could almost kiss her. "Katherine..."

Then the caped figure walked straight through him in an icy draft, as if it had just walked over his grave. He screamed.

He did not hear the German armoured car.

A few days later a young German soldier stopped Marie-Louise as she walked the small herd of Jersey cows back from pasture. He'd waited by the drystone wall near the cow shed, knowing roughly the time the girl came back in the afternoon.

As he waited for her, he looked down the gravel road toward the dunes, thinking about the night of the storm, the night he was out on patrol. Try as he might, he couldn't remember much about it at all. He'd fainted, so his sergeant had said. They'd carried him back to the barracks. But nobody in his squad would speak about it. If he asked questions they would avert their eyes, or conversation was abruptly changed; then eerie silences or, in one case, chain smoking and a nervous laugh. And no sense.

He got no straight answer about why he'd passed out from anyone, least of all his friends. All he'd got for his troubles, along with the others, was a severe bawling out by Major Kessler, with their weekend leave cancelled for a month. He remained at a loss to understand why.

As the girl brought the cows home, he could see that she had been crying. Her eyes were red-rimmed and puffy. She was pale, bereft.

He took off his helmet and put it on the wall, then he reached into the sidecar of the motorcycle. He wanted to return her father's belongings, found near where Mr. Dubois had been struck down and killed, to her.

A little nervously, he passed her the brass lantern, a ship's lantern. "It was your father's...I think it's quite old, ya?"

Marie-Louise stared at the lantern, then at the soldier, perplexed. She'd never seen it before and doubted if it was her father's. Then she started to cry.

The soldier looked around, unsure of what to do next, of what was expected of him. He tentatively moved his arm toward her, then awkwardly, he patted the girl's shoulder and looked out on a placid glassy sea.

Daniel Lillford

6: Burg's day

To say Bradley King stood out was somewhat obvious. Eighteen years old, at nearly 340 lbs, Bradley was hard to miss. He received his nickname 'Burger' in grade four. 'Burger King' stuck to him throughout elementary and into high school.

Wade Graves and Nate Shepard, the local shitweasels, were the boys who first started calling him it. It caught on with the other kids, as wicked nicknames often do, and it was Bradley's first lesson in the abject cruelty of little human beings.

Obesity ran in Bradley's family. His mother and father were both large. Some folk called them lard asses; nice people said big boned.

In grade eight Bradley knew things were getting bad when a structural engineer had to come to their house to check out the basement beams, some of which had started to sag and crack.

They had to install twenty-six jackposts. It was that or have the entire dwelling lifted and railway girders put across the top of the basement walls. His parents couldn't afford such an expense.

Bradley found this episode profoundly embarrassing, and not something he'd want spread around the small country town in which they lived.

The engineer also recommended replacing the wooden stairwell into the basement with concrete steps. Bradley noticed that the engineer had a slight smirk on his face when he suggested this to his father.

Tom King, who looked perpetually sad and beaten down by life, just shrugged, resigned to the merry-go-round of bad news. For Tom, it was just another nail in the coffin called "we can't afford that."

Not that it mattered to him in the end. He died in the stockroom at the grocery store, where he'd worked since leaving the same high school his son now attended.

Tom King, 42 years old, was on his lunch break when it happened. The Coroner's finding was that he had choked on the chicken sandwich he was eating when a small bone had gotten lodged in his throat.

A special casket had to be made, costing the family another two grand, reinforced and made of solid oak. Nobody, family or friends, put up their hands to be pallbearers. In the end it was four bodybuilders from the local gym who helped out for a small fee.

The size of a cemetery plot is nine by four feet. Fortunately, the King family plot was a double.

Grade nine was a tough year for Bradley. His father had died in August. His mother, Eileen, started what were to become numerous health concerns and, like the dutiful son that he was, he took it upon himself to look after her as much as possible, often skipping classes and accompanying her to doctor's appointments and hospital visits.

His grades began to suffer. Not the sharpest knife in the drawer, it was always a chore for Bradley to do well, but now he found himself struggling. There were days where he felt like he was drowning. On top of this was the ongoing bullying and general highschool nastiness that had accompanied each and every day he'd known since grade four.

Sometimes he felt there was little reason to continue on, when getting out of bed had become a mountain to climb.

In many ways his mother's medical problems, her reliance on him, had saved his life. She needed him. As the years went by she needed him a helluva lot.

~

The burglary did not go exactly according to plan, but it had started well enough.

Wade Graves found the bathroom window unlocked, as his best

friend, Nate Shepard, had told him it would be. So far so good. He slunk into the bathroom like a snake. His skinny frame dropped on to a rug near the sink.

He listened, straining his ears, and heard nothing. Nate's information appeared correct, nobody was home. Still, he wished his partner in crime wasn't serving time in juvenile detention at Waterville, and was here with him now. Wade didn't like working alone.

The house was fairly nondescript, a 1950s split-level bungalow, shabby and in dire need of some TLC, not the pride and joy it must've been all those rosy years ago when Middleton was a bustling Valley town. He moved from the ground floor bathroom along a hallway toward where he had been told was the living room that came off the right side of the kitchen.

A sound stopped him in his tracks. He listened hard, his eyes adjusting to the darkness and the shadows of night within the house. He breathed quietly, waited and listened, but heard nothing more. Moving quieter, ears pricked, he could hear distant traffic, probably coming from Main Street.

Wade remembered their conversation with every step he took. "They have no dogs. Fuckin' idiots! Told me, swear to god, first giveaway of a dealer's house is fuckin' pit bulls or rottis roaming about the property. Fair point, but dumb as fuck, eh?" Nate had laughed at his own joke.

"Beside the fridge there's this small cupboard that's sorta half-under the back stairs. No fuckin' idea where they go, doesn't matter anyway. Inside that cupboard, it's full'a kitchen stuff, there's this loose floorboard. Can't miss it. That's where they keep their stash. Money and shit's there. Easy-peasy."

Wade found himself standing in the doorway leading into the kitchen. Blue light from a window hit a sink area and a kitchen table; the hum of the fridge momentarily startled him.

He made his way toward the fridge, taking in the small stairwell beside it. The cupboard was as Nate had said.

He opened it quietly, using his phone as a flashlight. Gingerly, he removed baking trays and cooking utensils out of the way as quickly and as quietly as he could. He found the loose board and lifted it.

A plastic bag full of cash, thousands of dollars, stared back at him. Next to this bag was a smaller one full of amphetamines, Oxycontin and the like.

Wade grinned, excited. He wanted a cigarette and a piss all at the same time, but that would have to wait.

~

Bradley King locked up the stockroom at the supermarket, putting the keys in his pocket as he lumbered off toward the aisles that led to the front of the building. One of the young cashiers was saying goodnight to Betty White, the manager, who was starting to switch the store lights off section by section.

"C'mon, Bradley, haven't got all night!" she said, chuckling to herself as Bradley picked up the pace, his rolls of fat undulating like waves under his t-shirt.

"Sorry, Mrs White."

He grabbed his winter coat and a tuque from a peg near the office door.

"See youse tomorrow, Bradley."

"Goodnight, Mrs White."

She smiled, shook her head at her thoughts, and locked the doors behind him.

As he walked across the snow-covered car park, Bradley saw Betty's husband, Darryl, sitting in his truck listening to the radio, which was always tuned to a country station, waiting for his wife to finish her shift. For some reason Darryl reminded him of an old, faithful dog, the kind that smells, farts silently, and has a favourite couch it sleeps on. They shared a familiar look and nod.

Snow was gently falling as Bradley started home. He was so glad he had this part-time job, and was grateful that the owner, Mr. Baltzer, had offered it to him not long after Bradley's father had died.

Howard Baltzer was a kind old man with warm twinkling eyes, a

Daniel Lillford

gentleman who looked as if he belonged to a bygone era, a man who still dressed in three piece suits and wore a Fedora, whose shoes were highly polished, and gold cuff links always glinted from the cuffs of his perfectly-pressed white shirts. Baltzer didn't come to the store as often as he used to, retired as he was, but Bradley always felt that he was there somehow, like the building was part of him with his spirit watching over everything.

The store employees were the nicest people that Bradley had ever known. It was a joy to come to work there, a welcome reprieve from the toxicity of life in high school.

His graduation year was not going so great, and what with taking time out to care for his mother, he knew that his dreams of going to university and pursuing a career in teaching were looking decidedly bleak. He had no real savings to speak of and expected few if any scholarships. He had prepared himself for a gap year of working hard and saving.

Still, if there was one attribute Bradley King had over most of his high school year it was willpower and sheer, bloody perseverance. His life thus far had been like a skittle in a bowling alley. He'd been knocked down a helluva lot, but he always bounced back up.

~

Wade Graves was beside himself, he was so excited. He heard Nate's voice, which always sounded like he had a sore throat, ringing in his head: "Remember to put the stuff back like youse found it. No signs of a fuckin' break in, right?"

Wade replaced the old floorboard and covered it up with baking trays, cooking pots and utensils. He closed the cupboard, then made his way back toward the bathroom, plastic bags of money and drugs in hand.

The sound of a large truck gearing down rattled a window pane somewhere within and sent a shudder throughout the house.

He pushed the plastic bags out of the bathroom window, then hopped up as silently as before and slipped out, landing on the snow covered ground like a cat. Warily he took in the fenced side of the property, looked about, picked up the bags, then moved down the drive toward the street.

Searching left, then right, staying in the shadows, he walked with purpose toward the corner where a street light was flickering intermittently. He moved past a house that still had its Christmas lights blazing, red and blue blinking from bushes and leafless trees.

When he turned the corner, he froze. His car was under the roving flashlight of a police officer who was walking around it trying to look inside. The police cruiser was parked right beside it; he could hear radio chatter from within.

Wade muttered an obscenity, moved into the shadows and crouched low. It was cold and he gritted his teeth, afraid of them chattering. He tried to work out why the cop was so interested in his car. He'd been in no trouble recently. He watched through a picket fence, his heart beating fast. It was below freezing and he wanted to take a piss.

After a few minutes the police officer got into his cruiser and sat there for another minute looking at his computer before slowly driving off.

Bout fucking time, Wade thought.

He relieved himself against the fence, safe in the shadows, or so he thought. It was so cold the steam from his urine rose like a smoke signal.

Further down the street a dog barked. A light on a porch flicked on. Wade zipped himself up, ran to his car, his hand fumbled with the key.

An elderly woman walked out onto her porch, glancing toward where Wade had parked his car. She was wearing a worn plaid dressing gown and a Santa hat. Wade looked up and for a few seconds their eyes connected. He threw the plastic bags onto the passenger seat and got in. His black Honda Civic kicked into gear; with tires spinning in snow, he skidded off into the night.

Unfortunately for him, the police officer who had shown interest in his car had only driven around the block and was coming back down the street when Wade took off. The cruiser's lights and siren went into action and a pursuit began down School Street.

Daniel Lillford

When Wade noticed the police lights in his rear vision mirror he swore and hit the gas harder, turning left on Main, then left again on Commercial, fishtailing as he headed in the direction of Junction Road. He knew that if he was caught with drugs and cash he was for the high jump. There'd be no more slaps on the wrist in court. The last judge had hinted as much.

He noticed that the police car was gaining. He had to do something and fast.

~

As was his wont, Bradley made his way home via Rotary Park. He liked walking alone at night after work, no matter the weather. Most nights he'd walk through the park, often sitting on the old bleachers where he'd think, maybe have a conversation with the universe. Sometimes he'd just want to talk to his father again, talk about the day, school, work, and his mother's health.

He brushed some snow off the bleacher, sat and looked upward. It was cold and the night sky resembled the biggest display of static he'd ever seen. The snow was falling gently and steadily; the baseball and soccer fields looked like crisp white blankets. He stuck out his tongue and felt the snowflakes dissolving on it, smiling as he remembered *A Charlie Brown Christmas.*

The sound of an emergency vehicle broke his thoughts. He turned toward the siren, which was getting closer by the second. The flashing lights of a police car came heading toward the park from Marshall Street, and there were headlights from another, smaller car, a Honda, not more than a 100 yards ahead of it, both cars speeding toward the parking lot in the snow.

The smaller car entered the parking lot and travelled toward the bandstand where it momentarily slowed. Bradley was sure he spotted something fly from it toward the children's playground.

The police car, lights flashing and siren wailing, was in the parking lot quickly, chasing the smaller car around, both vehicles slipping and sliding in the snow like a couple of rally drivers. The police car fishtailed and almost collected the fence, giving the Honda a jump on the law as it headed back up Marshall Street.

Another police car appeared at the corner of King Street, and joined in pursuit of the Honda.

Bradley got up from the bleachers and walked toward the playground. The police sirens were now getting further and further away, up near the highway, he guessed.

A solitary swing creaked. The seesaw was half-buried, so too the little climbing frame and fort. Apart from a dog barking somewhere, the night was, once again, soft and gentle.

As he looked into the playground he recalled his early years, the snowball fights, building snowmen, soggy mittens, red cheeks and heavy boots, and his favourite teacher, Mrs Wentworth in grade three, who was always kind and patient. *She was a rarity in this place,* he thought, *a teacher who actually made a difference.*

The one friend he remembered with fondness was a Danish kid, Casper Hansen, who only spent a year at the school, then returned to Europe with his parents. Mostly he remembered being laughed at because he was fat. The soccer games he was allowed to play only if he was the goalie, for no other reason than to block the goal because everybody knows fat kids can't run. The taunts, the cruel jokes, the bitterness of a childhood robbed of so much that he couldn't explain, but robbed mostly of joy.

For a few seconds he wanted to spit out those memories, to yell, but it passed away like it always did. He controlled his anger, his bitterness, and he looked into the *Charlie Brown Christmas* world he stood in and watched his breath take the unhappiness away.

He had no more tears for the past. The children's playground resembled nothing more than a cemetery to him now, a place best left buried.

He found the plastic bag full of drugs beside the snow laden recycling bins. He saw nothing good or of value in it, so he stuffed the drugs into the bin compartment marked 'waste.' God knows there were enough addicts in this town without leaving temptation lying about. A third of the kids in his class were stoners, and grades 10 and 11 weren't much better.

He found the other bag resting beside the fence as he walked out of the park. When he brushed the snow off the bag his eyes nearly fell out of his head.

The money was all used bills. There were thousands of dollars in there.

He thought about his father, looked heavenward, smiled, turned and walked toward North Street, and home, where he knew his mother would be waiting up for him. They would have a cup of hot chocolate together, talk about the day; maybe watch some television.

Snow was falling heavier now. He found himself shuffling left, then right, shimmying, dancing like a bear might dance when nobody's looking. He felt light, as light as a feather.

7: Crystal Falls

After some vigorous shaking the cap flew off and ketchup machine-gunned the kitchen wall, hitting three porcelain ducks, a photograph of grandma, and murdering the man who had shaken it. Gerald Longmire looked like a squashed tomato. Gerald, his bald head liberally coated in sauce, sat holding the container in mid-air, contemplating the destruction and trying to maintain a serious disposition. A fatal lack of judgment under the circumstances.

There was a momentary pause of disbelief around the dinner table. Then the three Longmire children started to laugh. So, too, did Gerald's wife, Glenda.

"Well, this is a fine mess. Who didn't screw the cap back on properly, eh?"

His children, Tom, Carly and Isabelle, lost it. It was hard to take a man covered in tomato sauce seriously, even if he was their father. Glenda tried to quiet the kids down, but they were nearly falling off their chairs in mirth, and she was barely holding it together herself, when Gerald said, "Cut it out you lot, it's not funny!"

They laughed even harder. Gerald, annoyed, planted the ketchup container down on the table with a thump, which released another dollop upward like a surface-to-air-missile. He now wore ketchup all down the front of his shirt, and a sizable burst on his chin.

By this stage the children had forgotten about their chips and burgers. They were convinced they were in some sort of cartoon and their dad was the main character.

Their dog, an ancient lab mix, half-blind and nearly legless, started barking, sounding like it had bronchitis on top of all its other ailments.

Howls of mayhem filled the house and riotous tears of joy burst their banks. The old dog let one rip that stank the place out and nobody cared.

Gerald got up abruptly, his chair almost teetering over, and left the small dining room in a huff, slamming the kitchen door on his way outside. Windows rattled.

Glenda sighed and looked at her brood who were still giggling and wiping tears from their cheeks. She tried to stop herself from grinning but lost that battle.

"Daddy's funny, mommy," the youngest, Isabelle, said, her little face as red as an apple.

"Yes, yes, he's a funny man, your daddy."

Tom, the eldest, smiled at his mother, then ate a chip. He looked at the porcelain ducks. "They look as if they've been shot."

"So does grammy Longmire," Carly said.

"Daddy hasn't eaten his dinner, mommy, Isabelle said. Where's he gone?"

Glenda smiled, tousled the little girl's unruly curls. "Oh, I expect he's just gone to clean himself up, honey."

"No he hasn't. Naughty daddy," the little one said.

Tom smirked at his sister, then tore into his hamburger.

After he washed the ketchup off his face at the water barrel, Gerald went into the garage. He was still miffed at having been laughed at; but the more he thought about it the more he began to see it from their point of view. He realized that the thing he was really mad about was being embarrassed.

Ten minutes later Glenda made her way from the house, carrying a tray with his dinner on it. She found him under the hood of his pride and joy, a 1964 MGB, a two-door, racing-green sports car. He'd taken the tarp off it and it gleamed like a new dollar.

Glenda glanced at Tom with a smirk as she put the tray on the workbench. She waited for him to look up, which he did, eventually.

"Should eat before it goes cold."

He closed the hood with a neat click. "Thanks."

He tried not to catch his wife's eye, but she was having none of that. They looked at each other for a while, then he smirked. She smirked, too.

"Kids," he said.

"Humourless old fool, you mean."

She gently swiped him one across his bald pate, then she sat down on a paint-splattered stool at the end of the bench.

He took a few fries, leaned against the car.

"Tom and Carly have soccer practice in an hour, so don't forget."

"I won't," he said. "Thought I might take out the MG. Give it its first run for the year."

He looked at his wife, last year's summer dress clinging a little too tightly to her shape. She'd put on a few pounds, but so what, he loved what he saw. He loved his wife.

"What are you staring at?"

"Just you. A fine woman."

She smiled and looked into the garden. "Nice to be appreciated."

"Fishing for compliments?"

"That'll be the day," she said.

He watched her stand up, flattening out the sides of her dress, her hands pushing down at her thighs.

"Don't forget, soccer practice...Oh, and when you get back, there's a kitchen wall needs cleaning."

He sighed.

She smiled sweetly then walked toward the house. He watched her hips swaying and he thought about the first time they'd made love.

She stopped beside her rose garden and looked over a few of the plants before moving back into the house.

It had been up at Crystal Falls, a place where a lot of high school kids used to go, back in the day. A great place for a swim in summer, a wonderful waterfall.

He thought about taking her out in the MG, maybe on their anniversary in July, just the two of them, no kids. He'd make up a picnic, yeah, that's what he'd do. Make up a picnic and surprise her. Take the MG up to the Falls. Bring a bottle of wine, make a simple salad...No ketchup required.

Whilst admiring the MG and chuckling at his little joke, he

Daniel Lillford

reached over for some fries without looking at the tray, and dipped his fingers into a bowl of brake fluid.

8: Selma

The lilting Scottish brogue of Dr. MacGregor could still sting, and his words always came back to her in the witching hour.

"You have syphilis, Mrs Dorey."

The cold draft from the bedroom door lingered on her exposed arm as she looked at the gently ticking clock on the bedside table. An amber glass ashtray full of cigarette butts nestled beside her stack of detective novels, tortoiseshell reading glasses held together with electrical tape, and a tall glass with murky water that contained a set of well used dentures.

Selma thought about having a cigarette. It was 3:10 am. But she knew she would not get back to sleep if she did.

She moved her cold arm underneath the quilt that covered her small iron-framed bed. A tear bulged and then trickled out of the corner of her left eye onto the stained, caseless pillow. Under her breath she muttered, "You rotten bastard."

But she wasn't referring to Dr. MacGregor as a fatherless son.

Selma muffled a sob, thumped her pillow into shape, turned over and tried to get back to sleep, but when she closed her eyes all she could see was the stark Presbyterian look of judgment and admonishment in the doctor's eyes.

Her overweight Tabby meowed loudly and jumped from the top of the wardrobe onto the bed. It pushed its fat head into Selma's shoulder and armpit, meowing and turning in short circles. She knew the cat was agitated by the way it moved and flexed its paws.

Selma reached out and scratched the cat's head, speaking gently, "It's alright, Rex... It's all right..."

The luminous green eyes of the fat cat stared at its mistress. Then it curled up beside her and kept up a purr that went on for more than an hour.

The warmth of the feline, the softness of its coat, eventually lulled Selma Dorey back into sleep again. She snored with her mouth open, sounding like a tractor with misaligned tappets.

In the morning Iona McRae found her oldest friend standing on the dilapidated wharf across the road. Selma was staring out to sea; she didn't seem to hear Iona calling for her.

"Selma!? Lord dyin'...Are youse goin' deaf, Selma?"

The old woman walked gingerly onto the wharf, one small step at a time. Warped and lifted decking, rotted through in places, created jagged gaps showing the creosoted wooden pylons holding up what was left of the wharf. In the shallows below, a marine world of seaweed, crustaceans, molluscs and anemones blossomed in silence.

Carefully, Iona placed her walking stick, testing the grey boards, before moving the next foot forward.

"Selma, are youse alright? What is it?"

Selma managed a half-hearted smile, then her gaze shifted back toward the ocean. As Iona watched her steps, she made it close enough to look at Selma properly.

"Youse look all done in. What's wrong?"

Selma just nodded, but her watery eyes kept staring out toward Horse Island, with its colony of noisy cormorants nesting in spruce trees, trees that looked like charred matchsticks on a balding guano dome of rock set against the purest of blue skies.

"Lord dyin' Jeezus, what're youse doin' out here for? It's friggin' dangerous, woman!"

"Forty-five years ago, Iona...today. Youse remember? Knows I did."

Iona took a gulp of air that sent a minor tremor through her spindly frame, as if a bell had been rung against the insides of her rib cage. She put her hand on Selma's arm. "Come on, dear, I'll make youse a nice cuppa."

Selma removed her friend's hand, not forcefully, just firmly. Then she straightened herself and moved a few feet closer to the edge of the wharf. She looked down into the clear, shallow water.

She could see a large green crab scuttling across the rocks and sand.

"Still sees him lyin' there, in the water...Youse know."

"Yup. I remember," Iona said.

Selma turned toward the fish shack, her eyes scanning the remnants of what had once been a vital working wharf. A hollow hatch to the attic above gaped without its door; it was now a place frequented by barn swallows, not men. The wooden hoist was sun dried and gnarled, creaking in the breeze with a rusted pulley and rope encrusted in lichen. A heavy wooden block and tackle lay beside the paint-stripped main doors. Shingles were splayed, rotted out, or missing in patches along the sides of the building. Old glass buoys lay roped together in a large salt barrel beside the doors, their cotton netting all but bleached into granules of dust. A window stared out onto the cove, all the broken putty fallen from its grille, and a spider had made a web where a pane used to be.

Once painted in cream with green trim, the shack was now sandblasted back to the wood by decades of harsh Atlantic weather and neglect. The roof had visible holes where shingles and the tar paper underneath had been ripped away in great swathes; rough-hewn beams over 150 years old lay open to the elements. The chimney, more rust than steel, that once warmed the fish shack in those long winter months, now served as a vantage point for visiting seagulls and the occasional osprey.

"Poor Garnett," Selma said.

Iona said nothing, but her mouth tightened. "Well, he had it comin'...the dirty bastard."

Iona nodded and breathed evenly again. "Youse know he did, Selma."

Yes, she remembered that September afternoon in 1956. Iona McRae remembered it well.

Garnett Dorey, Selma's husband, had tied up his Cape Islander at the wharf with a fine catch of mackerel. It had been a good morning's fishing. After the fish had been boxed up in ice and loaded onto the truck, Guppy Cleveland and Albert Trask had driven off to the fish plant in Hubbards, leaving Garnett and Selma alone on the wharf. That would be the last time Garnett Dorey's crew would see him alive.

Iona arrived at the Dorey wharf dressed in her old jeans and work shirt, fully prepared to spend another afternoon helping Selma paint the fish shack. Since their earliest days together at the old, one-room schoolhouse in Northwest Cove, Selma and Iona had been firm friends, closer than many sisters. Inseparable, until Selma had got herself married.

Iona didn't much care for Garnett Dorey. She had never trusted him, and she'd heard plenty of stories about the man that made her concerned for her friend. But she never said an unkind word about him in Selma's presence…and she never mentioned the time Garnett had made a pass at her, not six months after he was married.

Garnett was Selma's choice. That's just the way things were. Like it or lump it. Still, she hoped he would not be at the fish shack, that it would be just her and Selma again, like old times.

She parked her Dodge Fargo on the shoulder of the road, then grabbed her Luckies and a small picnic basket that housed a few Schooner beers and some sandwiches. It was around 2 pm when she walked toward the fish shack with the smell of fresh paint wafting up her nostrils, and she was impressed by the amount of painting Selma had accomplished that morning. The afternoon sun bounced off the cream coloured shingles and the freshly painted dark green doors. Everything looked clean and bright.

She called for Selma, but received no answer, so she moved through the fish shack and called again, louder this time.

From the main doorway to the wharf, she saw her friend sitting beside an upturned barrel, staring into the water where the Cape Islander was moored. Selma's paint-splattered dungarees were curled up into her body. She appeared to be distressed.

Iona called her name again, but Selma kept her gaze on the water below the wharf.

Iona put the picnic basket down and moved quickly toward her. She glanced around to see if Garnett was about but couldn't spot him.

Her intuition crackled, instinct told her the worst before she knew anything at all.

She followed Selma's gaze into the sea. Garnett's blue-white face stared up at her, his body resting on the bottom of the cove, just below the stern of the Cape Islander. His arms were outstretched, he still had his work gloves on. There was some blood in the water.

"Oh, Jeezus..."

Selma was obviously in shock, sitting there all turned in on herself and shaking like gelatin.

Iona held her friend, who had started to cry, deep guttural sobs punctuated with a strange intake of breath that whined but stopped short of a screech. As she held and tried to soothe her, Iona saw an old wooden block and tackle on the wharf, not very far from Selma's bare feet. There was some blood on the boards.

She looked at Selma's tear-streaked blotchy face and bulging red-rimmed eyes and knew what had happened.

Her voice in her friend's ear was like breath on a feather. "Did youse hit him, Selma?"

Selma looked up into Iona's eyes and could only nod. Her face was a streaming mess of tears, sweat and snot.

Iona reached down and picked up the block and tackle by its rope, looked at Selma, who was still shaking and whining, then nodding to affirm what Iona was silently questioning her about. Without words, Iona moved across the wharf and around the corner of the fish shack. There was a small splash.

When Iona returned she was not carrying the block and tackle. She took a cigarette out of her packet of Luckies; her hand was not shaking when she lit up.

After a few quick puffs, then very calmly, almost nonchalant, she said, "Garnett must've slipped, fallen off the wharf, an' hit his head and drowned."

Selma looked at her, dumbfounded. She blurted, "No, Iona, Jeezus Christ. Youse saw yourself—"

"That's what happened. A terrible tragedy. It could've happened to anyone. An accident—"

"Iona, don't youse see? I, I hit him—"

"All I see here is an accident. Nothin' else. Do youse understand what I'm sayin' to youse, Selma?"

Selma muffled a sob, tears rolling down her face, staring at her friend.

Iona flicked her cigarette away, then gripped Selma's face between her hands and looked at her intently. "Listen to me. It was an accident, Selma. Youse have to see that. Think of your baby. The baby... That's what youse have to do. Leave the rest up to me."

She left Selma and went inside the fish shack, coming back quickly with a dead mackerel in her hand. She went to the cutting table, grabbed a knife and sliced the fish open, then moved to the edge of the wharf where the block and tackle had been and rubbed the purple-black blood and guts of the fish into the wood where drops of Garnett's blood lay. She made sure it was all smeared over, then she dropped the gutted animal near the salt barrel, stood on it and rode it under her foot toward the edge of the wharf, creating a greasy skid mark.

Selma stared at her. "Why'd youse do that for, Iona?"

"Don't want no police askin' awkward questions."

And the police never did. They treated Garnett Dorey's death as an unfortunate workplace accident. There was nothing to suggest otherwise. They took statements from the women and the crew. They retrieved the body.

The Coroner found the primary cause of death was drowning, coupled with a traumatic head injury, which he attributed to the deceased having hit his head on the boat whilst falling into the water.

Before Iona had called the police, she and Selma sat in the fish shack, holding each other. Selma was in a bad way, and Iona knew that she had to get her friend thinking straight again before the police started with their questions.

As Selma wept in Iona's arms, she remembered when they were at school together; when her mother had died, and when her father had told her it was best she went back to school rather than bawling around the house from morning till night.

She had gone back to school the day after her mother was buried, to please her father, and tried hard to be a brave little eight year old girl. The teacher, Mrs Hannam, who was normally very strict and uncompromising, melted upon seeing the child trying to tough it out in front of the other children whilst her heart was falling apart. She gave Iona the key to her own private sitting room, next door to the classroom, told her to sit with her friend away from all the others, to be quiet, listen, just be her friend.

Selma remembered crying herself to sleep in Iona's arms, and Iona never let her go nor woke her up. Not once. She just held her and stroked her hair. Selma thought Iona might have sung something, maybe it was a lullaby, but she couldn't remember.

When Mrs Hannam walked into the sitting room at school's end, she almost dissolved into a puddle. The little girls were asleep in each other's arms, looking like a Victorian picture Millais might have painted.

She closed the sitting room door behind her, grabbed her coat, muttered something quite out of character, and then walked to the child's home half a mile down the hill to give Selma's father a piece of her mind. A tongue lashing he would not soon forget, bereaved widower or not.

The day before Garnett's funeral, Selma told Iona what had happened on the wharf. They were sharing a few beers and some cigarettes. Iona had driven her Dodge truck down to Bayswater beach, and there they sat together on the sand, staring into the closing light of day.

It was also when Selma told her friend about being infected with a venereal disease, and she found herself crying again, only this time the tears spat out of her eyes in fury and hate.

"Good as told me I was a liar to me face," Selma said.

"He wouldn't go see no doctor then?"

Selma shook her head and swigged on her beer. "Nope. Said there was nothin' wrong with him, that it was me, that I needed my head looked at as well."

She took a cigarette out of Iona's pack of Luckies, and lit it with the dying embers of her last one. She pushed the dead butt into the sand and released a long line of smoke from her lips. "So I confronts him 'bout that tart he's been seen with, more 'an once down at Fox Point, youse know who I mean."

"Yup. Bet that went down well."

"Oh, yup. He went for me, all right. Nothin' unusual in that. Reckon he'd have brained me if I hadn't been so quick on me feet. Denied everythin', a'course. Didn't like that bein' thrown up in his face. Truth hurts, as they say. So I says to him, well I suppose Dr. MacGregor's wrong, that he don't know what he's talkin' 'bout, an' I'm wrong, because youse is always right. So maybes I caught the pox from off the toilet seat down at the Shore Club, eh? An' that bastard jest laughed. He laughed at me, thinkin' I was makin' some stoopid joke about it, as if I could ever make a fuckin' joke 'bout bein' diseased. An' the shame. Bein' pregnant, the horrible...I dunno, Iona, but, Jeezus, somethin' jest snapped in me. I saw red, an' I mean it, I actually saw everythin' turnin' red before me very eyes. Next thing I knows, I'm swingin' this block through the air...an' it hits him fair square on the back of the head as he was walkin' away, still laughin' at me. He falls down on his knees, dazed, like. Yup..."

Iona took the beer away from her mouth and looked at Selma quizzically. "Then Garnett, he fell off the wharf, right?"

Selma took a drag on her cigarette, shook her head, then exhaled. "Put me foot in the centre of his back, pushed, and over he went. An' he drowned."

Iona stared at Selma, as if she was looking at her friend in a strange new light. She reached for a cigarette out of pure nervousness, unsure what to say, if there was anything she could say. Her hand shook as she tried to light up.

Selma steadied Iona's hand and looked into her eyes."So now youse know, Iona. Now youse know."

The following February, Selma gave birth to a boy weighing less than five pounds. The child was diagnosed with congenital syphilis.

The two old women carefully threaded their way off the rickety wharf and started walking up the road in silence, Iona holding gently onto Selma's elbow. They moved past St. Cuthbert's

Anglican church, continuing up the hill. Selma stopped to catch her breath a couple of times, a wheezing rattle escaping from her chest. Iona, as was her wont, watched Selma with concern. Selma had never given up the cigarettes, unlike herself.

The church sexton, Philip Cottesloe, was repainting the cemetery picket fence, something he did every two or three years. He watched the two old ladies approaching, smiled, nodded and carried on painting.

They stood beside the grave of Garnett Dorey. But it was the smaller grave, more of a plaque really, that they had come to visit.

> Cain M. Dorey
> Born: February 10th, 1957
> Died: February 12th, 1957
> Safe in the Arms of Jesus

Selma knelt and brushed some leaves off the small plot and pulled out a few weeds near the edges. "Would've turned 44 this year," she said.

Poplar leaves swirled in a circle of gold as the wind whipped up, then died down again, scattering them against the fence. A downy woodpecker hammered away at a birch, a pair of blue jays shrieked and darted amongst the trees, and a red squirrel's klaxon whir momentarily filled the stillness.

Selma ran her nicotine-stained fingernails over the boy's name. "Couldn't have any more. Dr. MacGregor told me that. Said the disease hadn't been caught soon enough. Said it like it was all me own fault. Lookin' at me like I was Satan's own daughter with them hard eyes of his...Every month for four months, goin' into Hubbards for the penicillin; droppin' me drawers, bein' jabbed in the arse. Pregnant an' ashamed. Ridiculed. An' that nurse he had workin' there, that cold bitch from Halifax, starin' at me like I was not worth troubling over. Twenty years old, Iona, that's all I was, an' they had me marked as a pox-ridden fire ship, no questions asked. Like I never mattered, youse know. An' all the gossip an' the lies. Patient confidentiality, my arse. They spread bad news like manure on a field...Evil people, Iona, pure evil. God in heaven..."

Iona had heard this litany many times throughout the years, but she never interrupted Selma. She let her run her course as she would, as she had to.

Since the baby had died, Iona had seen a change in her friend. It was subtle at first, incremental, but it was there. It had gotten worse every year. Perhaps it was connected to the disease, what it had done to her, she did not know; but she had noticed a feeble-mindedness slowly taking over Selma's personality, an emotional instability, like a creeping sickness. It had almost obliterated the memory of that spritely young woman she had adored so much.

Sometimes she found herself having to turn away when Selma disappeared, like she often did these days, into those dark vaults of twisted reminiscence. After all, someone had to remain rooted in the present when the past clamoured in all its vehement futility.

Selma spat on Garnett's gravestone. "An' him, lyin' there with nothin' to say on his headstone 'bout what an adulterous whore monger he was, an' what evil he left behind..."

Iona took hold of Selma's elbow and gently helped her weeping friend to her feet. She hugged her.

As he painted the fence, Philip Cottesloe had heard fragments of sentences, but nothing clearly.

He looked through the slats and saw the two women sharing an embrace beside a grave. Two old ladies bundled together in yesterday's woollen overcoats. It made him smile. He thought to himself that whomever was buried there must have been well loved.

He thought for a moment he heard singing. A lullaby? No, it was just the wind.

9: One Sunday

Very few people were listening to Reverend Trotter's sermon at Holy Trinity. Sadly, it was becoming a habit, brought about by the priest's now-common refrain: "I was on the Internet the other day and—"

The gruff, sun-dried faces of the fishermen and their equally-gruff wives stared at their new parish priest, some wondering what planet he'd come from. Half the elderly congregation turned off their hearing aids; the other half reached for their Bibles, or started knitting. Some made for the bathroom. Joan Harnish would step outside for a cigarette, and Lester Croucher would go and sit in his car for ten minutes.

Reverend Trotter appeared oblivious to this as he rambled on about something totally unrelated to the Gospel reading. Most of the congregation could not relate to a single word that he said. It was as if he were speaking in a foreign tongue, strange technical jargon they did not understand or comprehend. Unfortunately for him, 95% of the aging congregation did not own a computer, had never owned one, and were not interested in purchasing one.

Since taking over the parish four months ago, Reverend Trotter had rarely been seen out in the community, and he hardly ever stayed at the vicarage, which he found smelly and damp, or so the sexton, Cyril Harnish, had said, and the word had spread.

The old vicarage on the shore road that had served so many priests over the decades now took on a sad and lonely countenance.

Stephen Jodrey, one of the youngest parishioners at 46, often wondered why Trotter had become a priest at all. His sermon was another abysmal effort in popular escapism. No substance, just sugar-coated pap. It insulted his intelligence.

Stephen shook his head and stared at his feet. On this, the 3rd Sunday after Pentecost, like so many Sundays since Trotter had taken over at Holy Trinity, Stephen wondered what the hell he was doing in church. On such a beautiful spring morning he could have been out pottering in his garden or making some repairs on his boat. It was a fair thought, given where Trotter had now decided to take his sermon:

"Now, if Jesus had possessed the technology of the Information Age at his fingertips, a website profile..."

Stephen Jodrey found himself rising abruptly from his seat, third pew from the back, then quietly walking out. It did not go unnoticed, except by the Reverend Jason Trotter, who was lost somewhere up his own virtual highway.

The sun was beating into the old Gothic doorway of the church. It was a glorious day. Stephen stood on the steps taking in the fresh breeze coming in off a plate-glass ocean.

The wooden door creaked open behind him and April Gates, his old elementary school teacher, came out, looking decidedly flustered. "Stephen."

"Mrs Gates."

She reached into her handbag and rummaged around for her car keys, her small arthritic hands shaking. "Another Sunday morning wasted," she said.

Stephen smiled. "You're not stayin' for communion, then?"

"No, I'm not. God forgive me. I miss Reverend King so much. This used to be my church..." She breathed hard, held her tongue, her tears, then forced a tight smile. "Have a good day, Stephen."

Stephen nodded. "And you, Mrs Gates."

He watched her walk down the road toward her car. He saw her take out a handkerchief from her jacket.

She was right, Reverend Gordon King was a priest to miss. A man who had thought the world of his parish; a man who did everything he could for his parishioners. Old school. Holy Trinity was always full when he preached, and he'd presided here for nearly 25 years. He was genuinely loved and looked upon with a great deal of fondness, and not just by the local Protestants.

It had been a terrible shock when he passed away so suddenly. Not old, at 64 he had many good years left, or so they had thought.

The strains of the offertory hymn "What a Friend We Have in Jesus" filtered outside, bringing with it Connie Finck's out of tune voice rising high above all the others in the choir.

Stephen smiled at his thoughts as he walked away from the church and crossed the road toward the beach. A bell gently clanged on a moored yacht. Seagull shadows cut across the sand as they glided in to land on the shoreline, where sandpipers skittered in small groups near the shallows. The smell of rotting seaweed stank out the beach and sand flies proliferated in their thousands.

He reached into his coat for a cigarette, then remembered he'd left his pack at home.

Careful not to get his good brogues caught by the incoming waves, he walked close to the line of fresh seaweed left by the tide.

Something big and rolled up in large strands of kelp caught his attention. Buzzing flies created a black mist all around it. Unnerved, he moved closer.

Two months back he'd been fishing off Ironbound Island and his nets had brought up a grisly find. He wasn't the only fisherman to experience this. Body parts were still washing ashore even after all these months.

When Reverend King had had a heart attack and died, Stephen Jodrey, though saddened upon hearing the news, was not surprised. The poor man had listened to and counselled so many of the local fishermen, shouldering much grief and anger. Throughout it all he had remained a beacon in their times of darkness.

The stress had to have worn him to the edge. After all, so many of the men had gone out there that night to help; that awful night when a passenger jet had crashed into St. Margaret's Bay. They had all gone looking for survivors. They had returned to their coves empty-handed, pale, grief-stricken, forever changed. There were no survivors.

That night still came back to Stephen in strange flashes of memory, like a faulty circuit chaser in his brain. Sometimes it was just a blur of lights and reflections, constant radio chatter, tears, a shared rum bottle and gaffs that poked into the carnage. It all felt so unreal now.

He remembered his Cape Islander bobbing in a sea of debris, the lights on the other fishing boats and the coast guard cutters, buzzing helicopters, all sweeping the dark ocean, everyone searching for a glimmer of hope.

Marty Johnson, one of his crew, a grizzled veteran who had served two tours in Vietnam, had looked at Stephen and called it right: "It's a sea of guts, bud. We ain't gonna find nobody out there. Not in one piece."

They found nothing whole, but they stayed out all night anyway, sweeping the area, searching until dawn broke. Some of the other fishermen couldn't handle what they saw, or what they found, and they turned their boats around and came home. Who could blame them? Even those like Marty, who had seen hell up close in war, broke down and cried like children. It was a tragedy, and it was bloody awful.

The days, weeks and months that followed the disaster were still taking their toll on the men and their families, their communities. Some marriages had crumbled, others remained simmering on the brink. Many had turned to drink or drugs, prescription and otherwise. Some cracked.

Nobody talked openly about those they knew to be suicidal, or their own stages of depression. Only Reverend King had waded into that quagmire. He was not afraid of the darkness. Those who, like Stephen, had sought spiritual guidance found, at first, a kind of uneasy solace in talking things out with him.

But it got better. It got easier. There was no judgment, just a caring man who listened well. The priest became a lightning rod for those who felt they were going under. Within a week of the disaster every fisherman in the parish who had been involved received his telephone number on a hand-written card that said, "Call me anytime. Day or night. I'm here. I'll listen."

And he was true to his word to the last.

"If we'd found jest one, jest one. It would have been enough...It would have been enough."

Stephen wondered if he wasn't kidding himself at the time as he remembered those words again. But Reverend King had listened, nodded and agreed with him, then said, "Any time you think you can't handle it, please remember I'm here, Stephen, I'm here for you and your friends. Tell them that. Make sure they all know."

That's what he was like. As Stephen stood on the beach he recalled a white-haired, elfin man standing in his dog collar and long black coat beside the Government wharf at 5 am, willing to talk to any of them as they started their day, to bless them, crack a joke, whatever. At lunchtime he could be found at the local diner, seated up at the counter with a coffee and a smoke, in the thick of it with the assembled plaid shirts and stained ball caps of working men.

As Stephen thought about the priest, he quietly said a prayer and looked upward into an almost clear blue sky.

Reverend King had the ability, or so it seemed in those early weeks of turmoil, to be in two places at once. He'd put up with a helluva lot more than most of the people around here would ever know. And they would never know how many lives he'd helped bend back into shape.

Stephen missed him. They all did. He was a decent man. Of late, he'd thought that perhaps they were all, part way, responsible for the priest's death. It was a pointless, guilty thought, irrational; he knew that, but it still cut him deep.

"Youse tell me, Reverend King, where the hell was Jesus that night, eh? An' where was God when that plane crashed into the sea an' killed all them innocent people? Why'd he let it happen, our merciful God, youse tell me that!"

Stephen's bitter, angry words came back to haunt him. He'd pounded on the vicarage door, out of his mind with his inner demons and lack of sleep. The words he'd spat out in a rum-tanked fury at a sleepy bewildered-looking priest in a tartan dressing gown, his hair like porcupine quills, glasses all lopsided, put on in a rush to get to the door.

The memory made Stephen ashamed. Waking the poor man after 2 am, and on a Sunday, of all days. "Jeezus, what a drunken fool I was," he murmured.

But Reverend King had brought him inside, sat him down in the kitchen, put the kettle on, offered him a cigarette, and looked at him with those dark thoughtful eyes. When he answered Stephen's anger, he spoke in a clear voice. He never raised his tone, he showed no annoyance, he just spoke clearly and plainly, said what he needed to say. And he said it in that cheerful Newfoundland voice of his that could cut through the crap of life like nothing else could.

"Stephen, I do not know why God allows such misery to occur. Truth is, I've never known nor understood horrors like Auschwitz, or slaughterhouses like The Somme, where so many of my own countrymen were sacrificed on the altar of war. And here, too, in this beautiful little part of God's kingdom, we're not immune from terrible acts of violence. Made all the worse because no-one survived...You ask why? Why indeed? Well, God knows, because I surely don't. I wish I did know "why", Stephen, truly I do. But I don't...So, is this the darkness to wallow in now, is it? A whirlpool full of anguish and hate? Oh, I know some find comfort in striking out in their rage, and why not? We all want answers and we want to hurt back because we're hurting. It's natural to blame God when answers are not clear, or simply not there at all. Sure the old fella's used to it by now. Though it's a bit like pissing in the wind for all the good it does anyone...When doubt rolls in like an October fog, it's easy to use anger as a convenient crutch of indignation. But it's a hollow staff to lean on, and it will break. And when it shatters, what do you grasp for then? The alcohol, the drugs? That's fool's gold, and a sure road to hell on earth. Then what's left? As a Christian, as a priest, I can only say this, and perhaps you will understand, if not the senseless arbitrary nature of death itself, then at least a loving merciful Christ...And, like all things in Christ's teachings, the lesson is always clear for those who are ready to listen."

The priest picked up his Bible from the kitchen table, opened it to Matthew, found what he was looking for, grunted, closed the good book, looked at Stephen, then recited.

> *But when he saw the wind boisterous, Peter was afraid; and beginning to sink, he cried, saying, 'Lord, save me.'*
>
> *And immediately Jesus stretched forth his hand and caught him, and said unto him, 'O thou of little faith, wherefore didst thou doubt?' And when they were come into the ship, the wind ceased.*

He smiled, scratched his head, got a cigarette out of his pack, leaned against the sink, lit up.

"You think I'm a drownin' man, that it?"

"I do, but you're not unique. Look around. Take a good look. That's right, even myself standing here. We all slip, Stephen; we all go under from time to time, some more than others; some more often than others. That's all. And it's no indictment on your character, perish that thought. All Jesus is sayin' is: here's my hand. I'm here. I'll help. I'll keep you afloat. Even when you doubt and your faith fails you, I'm still here and I'm going nowhere, and I'll save your sorry arse into the bargain."

He put the boiling water into the teapot, warming it before making a brew. Then he took a deck of cards off the shelf and reached for the crib board. "So, now I'm awake, we'll play a few. Least you can do after pounding my door to kingdom come, scaring the living shite out of me, you know that?"

Stephen moved away from the pile of seaweed as he reached into his coat.

"Penny for your thoughts, Stephen?!"

Ailish Constable's Irish voice took Stephen right out of his thoughts. He removed his hand from his coat as she walked toward him. He felt nervous, distracted.

"Ah, Ailish. So, the service is over."

Ailish raised her eyebrows. "It is, yes. Another Sunday morning gone to pot."

He nodded. Stephen liked Ailish's sense of humour. She always shot straight with a barb.

Ailish belonged to the choir, one of the eight regular members, and the youngest at fifty. She was also the only member with any musical knowledge. Not that it had helped much, as they were a lovable choir of pig-headed mavericks who did what they liked.

"You walked out. I saw you," she said.

"Yup. Guilty. Think I'll, I'll stay away for a bit. Not getting anythin' out of bein' here any more, youse know, nothin' spiritually..."

"Uplifting?"

He nodded and frowned. "Yup. Somethin' like that."

"Well you're not alone. Plenty feel as you do. It's a shame. All the same, they were hard shoes to fill, you'll agree? I feel a bit sorry for him, terrible thick though the man is. Still, it's not a club. It is a church, after all. You must do what you feel is right. Could always join us, the choir, have a few laughs. We all drink and tell dirty jokes. Have a gas time. Besides, we could do with a few more male voices; Charlie's pipes aren't what they used to be, and Kent is more a soprano than a tenor, bless his sweet soul..."

He grunted. "Not on your life."

"No harm in asking." She smirked, then looked out to sea.

He found himself staring at her face, her crinkly blue eyes, high cheekbones and fine white hair that must have been very blonde when she was a girl. She was a striking woman, and her voice had always had a strange calming effect on him. After his marriage had broken up some twelve years before, he'd found it very difficult to talk to women, to even be around them. He felt clumsy and shy. Old. Unsure of himself. Unsure of them.

Ailish put him at ease, effortlessly so. But he wasn't lonely for company like she was. His first love remained the sea, that was where he was most at home, where he felt sure of himself.

She pointed toward the mass of seaweed and buzzing flies. "Stephen, what's that over there?"

"Dead seal. That's all."

She looked at him sharply, searching for a second, then she grinned, squeezed his arm. "Well, I shall miss you, Stephen. But I guess I'll see youse comin' back, as they say here."

He nodded and looked away. "Yup. See youse comin' back, Ailish. Take care."

She reached over and gently kissed his face, then turned away.

He watched her walk off down the beach, her tweed cape and green woollen scarf floating behind her. She crossed onto the shoulder of the road, turned around and waved, walked on. He raised his hand but didn't wave back, just watched her move on up the road toward her cottage. He felt his cheek where she'd kissed him, then he reached into his coat and took out his phone.

Reverend Trotter stood in the church doorway trying to find his keys to lock up. He was annoyed. Most of the congregation had left the service as soon as the last line of the recessional hymn had concluded. In fact, he could have sworn that there was almost a stampede to leave Holy Trinity this morning. Not one of the faithful had said anything about his sermon, which he thought was one of his best. There was no doubt in his mind that these country parishioners were a little odd; a little backward and ungrateful. He found them a brusque unsophisticated lot. Peasants.

As he walked toward his van he hoped that the Bishop would grant his request to leave this dull place and take over another parish that had become vacant closer to Halifax. To be back in civilization and not stuck out here in the boonies.

The sound of a speeding car made him look up in time to see an RCMP cruiser, lights flashing, come to an abrupt halt at the beach not 100 yards from where he stood. He could see another police car tearing down the coast road from the opposite direction, it had its lights flashing but no siren turned on.

The first police officer got out of his vehicle and walked with purpose across the sand toward where Stephen was standing.

Reverend Trotter got in his van. He was quite convinced that the police were arresting some criminal. And he said to himself as he drove off in the direction of Halifax, *The sooner I'm out of this backwater, the better.*

Daniel Lillford

10: Roads back

The Atlantic heaved under a violent westerly, belting the seawall on St. Ouen's Bay with menacing waves that shot spray 30 feet into the air with the savagery of clashing symbols, leaving saltwater to hit the road like a shower of bullets. The coastal road was awash, but it was not flooded, not yet.

Across the road the wind whipped Maudie Sinclair's dark hair about her face as she tried to picture again the old granite farmhouse that had once stood on this corner. A house blandly known as Corner House. During the war, when the Germans occupied the island, they called it Marlene's House, after her grandmother, Madelaine.

She leaned on the old drystone wall, or what was still left of a wall that had once surrounded two sides of the house, and tried to imagine this place when no real roads existed; a rural crossroads where tracks were made by horses and carts, cows going to pasture, and by men going down to the sea.

Then came the first pieces of machinery. The tractors, her grandfather's old Bedford truck, the same one he used to cart seaweed, or *vraic* as the older island folk still call it, from St. Ouens Bay to the farms, to spread on the fields as fertilizer for growing Jersey Royals, arguably the finest potato in the British Isles.

The pre-war black-and-white photograph Maudie held in her hand reflected a lost world, another time. The sandy road in the picture was all the more conspicuous for its lack of tarmac, buttressed by thick prickly gorse bushes, ribbon-sharp marram grass, and the ever-present dunes where she'd played all along the Five Mile Road. In the 1960s, and especially through the eyes of a child, it had been a wild place. An Enid Blyton world, and Maudie's very own adventure playground.

Sadly, it was wild no more. All gone. The savage sea notwithstanding, the landscape looked oddly manicured, even tamed. No, it was not as she had remembered it.

In the photograph her grandmother was standing at the front of the farmhouse, a flowered pinafore covering her thin cardigan and skirt, a beret on her head, thick lumpy stockings, and chickens at her feet. A Jersey-French farmer's wife.

Maudie barely remembered the old lady, and when she did it was to recall a woman with fierce, piercing blue eyes, snow white hair, a scowl and a quick temper. She possessed a discontented face.

However, it was the house in the photograph that held Maudie's interest, like a mirage of memory, as she tried to unlock a time she wasn't sure of anymore. It was an ugly grey building, squat, hard-edged, all granite. Windows that did not welcome. A door that did not smile.

The lush edges of the mini-golf course stared back at her. A red flag flapped and thwacked violently against its post on the green. The sand bunker was where the old cow-shed had been. She remembered her mother telling her that the farm dog, a pointer called *Jacques*, would never go into the cow-shed. It would sit outside and growl. The cats never went in there either. She never learned why.

Annoying beeping electronic bells carried in the wind as the hire car door opened and Mark climbed out. He pulled at his coat collar, glancing briefly at the turbulent sea hitting the seawall across the road, and walked quickly to where his wife was sitting.

He put his arm around her, raising his voice to be heard. "You'll catch your death in this wind. C'mon, Maudie, get inside the car."

She smiled at him as the wind grabbed at her hair and the salt spray stung her face. She showed, him the photograph, then pointed. "That was where the gravel pathway to the front of the house was. I used to catch fire beetles beside the water barrel over there."

Mark nodded, stamping from one foot to another like a man in need of finding a convenience, his teeth chattering as he thumped his hands together. "Can we discuss this in the warmth of the car, please? I'm freezing my nuts off here!"

She laughed as he moved quickly with her across the road to the car. Thunder rumbled somewhere out at sea. The sky looked vomitous.

The warmth of the vehicle took the chill out of her hands. She felt her circulation returning. Mark flipped on the wipers by mistake, the rubber scraping the dry windshield and sounding like a protracted fart. He switched the wipers off and stared at the golf course.

"Can you imagine the uproar if some darn fool dared to pull down a 17th-century farmhouse in Canada? Holy shit…"

Maudie's face tightened. She shook her head. "There would be that all right. Different story here, or it was back then. Ah, Jersey is all about money. Always has been. The parish authorities had the gall to say that the house was in the way of the flight path to St. Peter's airport. And that was the excuse they used to see it was demolished."

"Kidding me?"

"Nope. It was a crock, of course. I know the National Trust people were very upset, but by the time they knew anything about it, the place was already levelled. It was quietly done. The wrecking crew came in at night. One of the big farmers around here was behind it, so my mother always said. Usual story, friends in high places, greased palms. Don't forget, my grandparents only leased the land; it didn't belong to them, so they had no say. They were just poor tenant farmers…Anyway, grandma hated the house, so maybe it all worked out for the best."

It started to rain hard now. Large splatters hit the car like stones.

"Why did she hate the house so much?"

"She was very unhappy here. I've told you that before. My grandfather, he…Well, let's just say it wasn't the greatest of marriages. And the farm barely made a dollar. Always a struggle. The scenery aside, their life out here was far from idyllic. She drank, too. I never knew, of course, I was just a kid, but my aunt Agnes told my mom.

When she was cleaning up after grandma died, she found red wine bottles hidden all over the place. A lot of them were half-empty. Squirrelled away for rainy days...Maybe days just like this one. Who knew? Her children sure as heck didn't have a clue. But it must have been going on for years. I guess grandma did a lot of things on the quiet. That's what makes it all feel so bitter...Even now, after all this time, I don't know why I should feel anything about this. It was such a long time ago. It was just a small part of my childhood, that's all. I was a little girl here, then my folks emigrated to Canada. It's not relevant to who I am now, or our life in Nova Scotia. And yet, it clings, you know...It clings. I wish I knew why. I wish I knew why it makes me feel so sad."

Maudie's smile trembled momentarily. Her eyes became cloudy. Mark flipped the wipers on. Ugly weather was tearing up the landscape, the wind buffeting the parked car and the rain teeming down on them with so much racket it was like they were sheltering under a corrugated shed.

"She must've been very lonely," he said.

"Yup. Lonely and trapped. Big old drafty farmhouse, middle of nowhere. She didn't drive, never learned. Hard to believe now, this island seems so small when you're driving around it, but back then the only roads around here were dirt tracks. Sandy gravel roads. There was no bus service. That was years away. There was no electric light, no telephones. In the 1930s my mother walked five miles to school every day, that was after she'd helped to milk the cows and put them out to pasture. Poppy died in 1967, so grandma was left here by herself for almost another decade. Her five children, all the grandchildren, were gone, scattered throughout the world. Some in England, Australia, Canada...the pink bits on the map. Shit, I'd have taken up drinking, too."

"You paint a bleak picture, Maudie."

"Just the way it was."

Maudie shrugged and stared at the rain pelting the landscape. She wished now it had been a sunny day, like August days used to be in Jersey. A warm day when the sea is gentle and the breezes are light. Days like she remembered when she was five years old, a girl on a mission, tea-tin in hand, her little brother David, by her side, and fire beetles to be collected. Or simply playing in the dunes, looking for the little people grandfather always said lived out there. These were the long hot Sundays of summer.

And Sunday was always visiting day at the farm. Her mother and grandma inside the house, sharing a cup of tea, speaking Norman-French, the local patois. Poppy would be with her dad in one of the sheds, working on an engine together or shifting potato boxes.

She wondered now how her grandmother must have felt when her parents told her they were leaving Jersey for Canada, knowing there was a good chance they might never see each other again. Which is what happened. Her parents weren't so young when they had left the island, looking for a better life.

As Maudie dwelt on these thoughts she felt strangely sick and empty.

Mark pressed a button and the radio came on. An early Beatles song was playing. He hummed along to it as he started the car, smiled, leaned over and gave his wife a peck on the cheek.

"It was haunted, too, the house," she said.

Mark reversed the car back onto the road. The wipers were working overtime. "Jeezus, I feel like I'm in a goddamn submarine, not a car!"

"There were rooms nobody went into. My mom always said something bad had happened there a long time ago. She hinted at a murder, and I know she was frightened of the cellar. Refused to go down there. Aunt Agnes wouldn't tell me anything either, but she always shuddered whenever I brought up the subject of ghosts."

"Surely you don't believe in all that nonsense?"

"I keep an open mind."

She thought to herself it was probably not the best time to tell him about the fairy road that ran through the dunes.

Mark sighed. "Best to stay away from all that superstitious crap. Can you believe this weather?"

"At least she got her wish..."

"How's that?"

"On her deathbed, Aunt Agnes and uncle Michael, they heard

what she said. Pretty much her final words: 'When I'm gone I hope they burn this place to the ground. It has brought nothing but misery.'

"She said that? So, she died in that house?"

"Uhuh...Well, they didn't burn it, but they bulldozed it. October, 1974. Built the golf course."

Mark grunted, his burly chest pinned against the steering wheel as he stared hard, trying to see the road through the windshield. He turned the car down the Valle de la Mare, driving slowly into the curtain of rain. "Think your gran might've liked golf?"

Maudie looked at him askance. He grinned. She punched him on the arm. Then she laughed.

Daniel Lillford

11: Echo

At first he thought it was snowing. Flurries in June? Not unheard of, but highly unlikely on such a beautiful day. On closer inspection, wearing his glasses now, he saw thousands of dandelion seeds blowing about the garden. The fortune-teller plant was casting out her wisdom into the world on the wind.

"Hello. It's been a long time, I know. How are you?"

He stared at the screen, somewhat gobsmacked. It was a voice from the past on Messenger. For a moment or two he found it hard to believe. The last time they had communicated was via letters, handwritten letters, in the mid-1980s, when she had gone to England to study and they, over a period of some years, had lost touch. That was nearly forty years ago. He'd often wondered why, but had always put it down to the tyranny of distance, work commitments, then marriage, children, life. He looked at her name and smiled. Like him, she would be nearing retirement age now, but when he thought of her she remained in her twenties.

He was about to reply but stopped himself. Instead, he made a cup of tea, went outside and wandered about the garden. The dandelion seeds had lessened and the wind had dropped. He thought about the cords of wood he had to get into the basement, and the following year's wood he was still to order. Her face kept coming back to him.

She had very bright blue eyes, kind eyes, an almond-shaped face, and thick, unruly blonde hair. She was small, no taller than five feet, and compact. Her skin was pale, blemish-free, almost translucent. She wore glasses, silver framed glasses. Yes, she was beautiful, but not aggressively so. Hers was a quiet beauty.

He remembered her stillness, or was it shyness? She always

seemed centred, observant, as watchful as an owl. A woman who didn't miss much.

He couldn't remember where they had met. Probably some cafe. Everyone met in cafes back then. When she smiled, he thought she had something of Marilyn Monroe about her face, like a shadow crossed over and the movie star was smiling at him through her. It had unnerved him at first.

They became friends, but he never really understood why. He liked being with her, he enjoyed her conversation, and he preferred to just listen to her talk, that sweet lilt she had, her northern voice. But he never felt her equal, and often he was so clumsy around her, like a buffalo sitting down to dinner with an otter. She was accomplished, whereas he remained a struggling, poor artist with barely five bucks to his name, and no real prospects beyond hopes and prayers.

She had a boyfriend, another artist as it turned out, a screen printer or sculptor, he couldn't recall. He remembered meeting the fellow a few times, and of course he was a nice guy; there was nothing to hate. He hid his feelings of jealousy at the time, put on a smile and pretended. He was good at pretending. When they happened to be all together he soon found reasons for departure, being the extra spoke in the wheel, so to speak.

Once, when he had left them at some cafe or other, he observed from the safety of the shadows as she snuggled into her fella and they kissed lovingly. He remembered how his heart sank, knowing that she and he would never be more than friends. Plutonic.

He respected their friendship and would never put it in any jeopardy...and yet he had tested it, he had provoked it.

It was to be the last time he ever saw her, though of course he didn't know that at the time. Thinking about it again made him feel kind of sad. An odd feeling of loss that he couldn't quite explain. Absurd, really.

If it had been a crossroads, then he had failed miserably to see it. Sometimes chances are like that, ghosts that pass one by, a banging door in the emptiness of a house without a breeze to be felt. One staggers about, wondering where the noise came from whilst standing in the door frame, looking for answers. Just another fool with the lights on, but nobody home.

She had this quietude, this cool inviolable border about her. *Strength*, he thought. Was it that that frightened him away from her?

He had admired her, more than he could put into words, and when he did try to express himself, he often found himself looking away from her, half-afraid that he wasn't making much sense or, worse, appearing like some idiot as he babbled about his latest adventures in the theatre. He had wanted her to love him as he quietly loved her. If only he'd had the guts to spit that word out when he could have and told her plainly.

He wondered if he had ever really relaxed with her; but he knew that he had, even if it was for only three minutes at a bus stop in a city now lost in the shadows of time. He had wanted to follow her to Europe, and had contemplated it seriously.

He thought about her letters again, and couldn't remember why he'd never gone, never visited. Had she dissuaded him from coming over; was it because of some other entanglement? He didn't know. Too long ago.

Why, after all these years? Why search him out now?

He tried to remember more as he walked around the beautiful garden his wife took so much pride in. The roses this year were showing great promise, with early buds aplenty. Bird chatter filled the air. Bees moved from the delphiniums to the lupines and flox, a joyous cacophony of industry. This small piece of paradise was a lifetime away from those dreary grey city streets of his youth, of her youth, and one half-forgotten autumn.

As he stared at the river, his mind travelled with it down to the sea, as if all his thoughts were boats; Irish currachs, Viking longships, birch bark canoes, yellow submarines, each tiny wave taking a thought into the ocean of thoughts of all the could-have-beens in life. That realm where Morpheus sleeps and holds one's dreams like so many letters lost in the mail.

He had said goodbye to her at a bus stop near a large university, in the autumn of 1984. He had looked into her eyes, found courage, taken off her glasses, swept her up into his arms and kissed her. It was mid-afternoon, in public, and he did not care a damn. Their bodies close for a moment in leather jackets, woollen pullovers and faded blue jeans; close for a moment in months of longing to be close but scared of waves, afraid of being swamped, drowned in feelings, tossed into the uncharted, castaways before the end of the world. She had melted into him and he had realized then, too late, that she too could fall. He knew then how much of a fool he had been, and he also knew he had missed the bus.

Someone once said "youth is wasted on the young." He smiled at the wisdom of that quip as he watched his longship disappear into the sea, into that fog bank called memory.

Somewhere, perhaps in a box in the attic, he'd kept some of her letters. He didn't know why. He wasn't even sure he would ever read them again, but he remembered how happy they had made him feel when he saw the airmail letters with stamps from Europe sail through his door. The simple joy of handwritten communication. Simpler times.

When one arrived he would take her letter to a favourite Italian cafe. A thread of images bled on the page in ink, as fragile as parchment left in the rain, weathered by loss and distance, forgetfulness; the longing, the work, study, the lovers and the dreams. Sometimes she wrote to him a little bit drunk, alone in her room in some English university on the other side of the world, and he could feel her loneliness, even touch it. Another coffee or two, more cigarettes, pages read and reread. Then he would reply.

Compose.

"My dearest..."

He looked through a portal into the past, into a world that does not exist any more, a world that was fleeting at best even then.

When letters stop there is an emptiness, like the sadness of walking through a loved apartment one last time, all the empty rooms where voices echo, dancing with so much dusty remembrance. The thread is broken, and it would take the folly of Orpheus to find Eurydice again, knowing, with the benefit of hindsight, how sadly that story ends.

As he stood on the riverbank he caught sight of a young man he once knew.

He saw this young man sheltered within his old, beaten-up leather jacket, full of badges and patches, his ripped Levis, with a cigarette hanging from his lips. The young man was smiling, but he was unhappy. Pretending again.

He watched himself sink his hands into his jacket pockets and hunch into that cold autumn afternoon, moving away from the bus stop beside the university. He half-turned, waved; then he was gone. She was smiling, holding her glasses.

"Hello. It's been a long time, I know. How are you?"

Ghost Breezes

Daniel Lillford

12: Pink

When Joan Hennigar discovered her husband's secret, she was shocked. It was, however, a natural reaction. After all, it's not every day that a wife comes home early from work to find her spouse dressed up in her gold lamé miniskirt, lime green silk blouse, fishnets and heels, wearing her makeup and dancing to the disco queen, Donna Summer.

Joan flung the front door open and Dougie Hennigar found himself sailing through the air. His first thought was about his neighbours, the Denismores, and what they might see or think, not the brute strength of his wife's throwing arm, nor indeed her angry words, as he rolled arse over kettles on the hard October lawn.

"It's over! I'm finished with youse!"

She slammed the door shut with such ferocity that a hanging basket full of geraniums slipped its chain and fell, bouncing down the porch steps scattering plants and soil everywhere.

Dougie picked himself up, a little groggy on the pins, and sheepishly looked around, hoping nobody had witnessed what had just happened. He gathered up the skirt, pulling it as far down his hairy thighs as it would travel, covering the red garter attached to the stockings that now had a ladder in them. The white high-heeled shoes he'd somehow jammed his plate-sized feet into fell sideways. He stood staring at the house, wondering how he could get back inside to get changed…and how he could possibly explain himself to his wife.

Joan abruptly threw open a window and started tossing out old LPs. A Barbara Streisand record came at him like a Frisbee, hitting him full in the chest and knocking him sideways. He was glad he was wearing his wife's G-cup bra stuffed with tissue paper. More records came flying out of the window in rapid succession.

"Jeezus, Joan! This is so unnecessary—"

"Shut up, you freakin' disco pervert!"

Judy Garland's Live at Carnegie Hall whistled past his head, followed quickly by The Bee-Gees Saturday Night Fever, Donna Summer's Love to Love You Baby, and The Very Best of KC and the Sunshine Band.

"I've been a fuckin' eejit! All these goddamn years..."

"Joan, please, let me—"

A Peter Allen album whipped across and almost took him out at the knees; Earth, Wind and Fire's September knocked the head off a garden gnome.

"There! That's all your fruity music out of my house for good! I should've listened to my father. He always said that any man who didn't like Johnny Cash was a cocksucker!"

The window slammed shut and the bamboo chimes rattled like gobbling turkeys. Dougie stared down at broken vinyl, empty sleeves and the covers of some of his favourite LPs.

Stewart Denismore looked through his kitchen window and wondered who the big, brightly-dressed woman was standing outside the Hennigar house. He thought she was probably a friend of Joan's, one of her co-workers from Corrections.

"Walks like a fisherman. Lordy, imagine that thing on top of youse," he muttered to himself.

As he trudged along the shoulder of the road heading toward where his sister lived in Southwest Cove, a good mile from his house, Dougie soon realized that fishnet stockings weren't meant for hiking in the great outdoors. Goosebumps as big as warts were rising out of his flesh. He was glad of the wig, a long blonde one he'd picked up at Value Village some months before. It at least was warmer than a tuque.

A metallic blue Chevy Cheyenne truck hooted emphatically at him as it drove past. Someone leaned out of the passenger window and yelled something lewd. He vaguely recognized the culprit.

The white high heels were not helping, so he stopped and took them off. Better to brave bare feet on the gravel than risk a twisted ankle.

As he walked toward the Ocean Swells Community Centre he prayed that the car park was empty and nobody was about...Prayer answered!

He breathed gentler...until Larry Dauphinee's beige Datsun, with its faulty muffler, growled and slowed up alongside him. Dougie knew then that his day had just gotten worse.

The bat-like features of Larry leered over his steering wheel. He was almost salivating. "Give youse a lift, sweet...heart..."

The look on Larry's face went from lust to bust in seconds flat. Dougie figured he'd noticed the moustache. "Jeezus H...Dougie Hennigar?...Oh, my fuck..."

Larry didn't wait for an explanation. His foot hit the pedal and the "Shitty Dat", as it was known, squealed, leaving five bucks worth of rubber on the road and a cloud like gun smoke in its wake. Dougie knew it would now only be a matter of hours before Larry Dauphinee's renowned shit-spreading abilities covered the county, and his life would be dirt.

Joan Hennigar was still sobbing on the telephone as she talked with her oldest friend, Muriel McLeod: "—Donna Summer, I ask youse, Muriel...Donna Summer! Jeezus wept..."

Muriel McLeod was a little unsure how to console her friend. If she hadn't been still at work, she'd have barrelled on over there to be a shoulder to cry on. "Where's Dougie, now, Joanie?"

"I don't friggin' know! Jeezus, Muriel, to be honest, I don't friggin' care!"

"He take the truck?"

"Nope. It's still at the garage, that's why he was home...Playin' dress-up in my things, wearin' my makeup an', an' dancin' the day away to Donna fuckin' Summer..."

Muriel heard Joan sob loudly and she wished she was there with her. "Oh, now, c'mon, hon, try to be brave. It'll all work out, you'll see..."

"Don't see how. My husband's one of 'em crossdressin' disco-bunny freaks'a nature. An' how long's it been goin' on, eh? Ask yourself that, Muriel McLeod, how long's this perverted business been goin' on under me own roof?"

Muriel couldn't answer that question. She was just a receptionist, not a psychiatrist or a clairvoyant.

When Dougie's sister, Maxine, saw her younger brother standing in her driveway, she didn't bat an eye. Though she did wonder about his taste in clothes. She emptied the wheelbarrow of leaves and filled another orange garbage bag. "Douglas. How's she goin'?"

"Oh, youse know, she's goin', Maxine, she's goin'...and gone, guess."

"Joan kicked you out, huh?"

Dougie nodded, shrugged, and looked lost.

"Better come inside. I'll get you some of Gordon's things...You should know that that skirt is butt ugly."

"Yup, well I wasn't exactly spoiled for choice."

He followed his sister into the house.

When Gordon came home later that afternoon, he found Dougie and his wife sitting out back with coffee and cookies. He recognized his old university windcheater on his brother-in-law as he gave Maxine a peck on the cheek. Although Dougie had had a shower and cleaned off most of the makeup, he'd missed some eye shadow.

Gordon smiled and looked over his spectacles. "Humorous rumours are rife down at the Hubbards supermarket. A strange tale is afoot regarding the sighting of a large blonde woman with facial hair, dressed in a short yellow skirt and fishnet stockings, last seen wandering the 329 an' heading this way."

Dougie grunted. "Sounds like more Larry Dauphinee horse shit to me."

"You got it. He's spreadin' it far an' wide to anyone who'll listen."

"Such a detestable weasel of a man. He makes my skin crawl," Maxine said.

"Yup. He's a piece'a work. But what were you thinkin' big guy, eh?"

Dougie shared a confused look with his sister, then looked at Gordon. "What're youse talkin' about, Gord?"

"He knows, Douglas. Gordon knows. You know...?"

"Gord knows what?"

"Lord dyin' Jeezus, stop bein' so goddamned thick! I told him...About you! Years ago. Okay, I broke my promise. I was always lousy with secrets. And don't look at me like that, Douglas, it's not exactly a secret any more now, is it? Everybody knows. Well, almost everybody. Look, try to see this in a positive light. No more hiding in the closet anymore, so to speak."

"She's right. Listen to your big sister. Maxine says you've been doing this, this crossdressing thing, since you were a kid, right? Not that it matters. Doesn't bother me. Vive la difference an' all that jazz."

Dougie looked at his sister in disbelief.

Maxine stared back. "What? What've I done wrong now?"

"C'mon you two, be adults. Besides, Larry Dauphinee has as good as named the large man in the yellow skirt. So, me old trout, it's all over Lunenburg county by now. Or will be by tomorrow. The thing that gets me, Dougie, is how come Joan never cottoned on? Or did she know? D'you think she knew?"

Dougie shrugged, took a swig of his coffee, stared into the garden. Gordon went to say something and a look from Maxine stopped him short.

A chickadee landed on the table, chirruped quite loudly, then tentatively picked at some biscuit crumbs. Dougie put out his hand and the little bird jumped into his palm, chirruped again, then flew away.

"Maybe she just pretended. Easier that way...I dunno. I have no idea. Never had the balls to tell her. Reckon if I had she'd have thrown me out anyway. Some things I guess, between husband an' wife, oughta remain in the closet. Christ, it wasn't as if I did it every day, it was only once in a blue moon. Still, glad Sandy and Kyle were at school."

"What're you goin' to do?"

"Well Gord, not much I can do now, is there? Move out...Wasn't given a helluva lot of choice in the matter. Suppose I should try and see that in a positive light, too, eh? Jeezus...Just worried about the kids hearing stuff, gettin' teased at school, that sorta shit. You know how it goes. All those assholes on the Facebook an' whatever else the gossips use these days."

Gordon poured himself a coffee. "Right. Never thought of that."

"They'll survive," Maxine said. "Kids bounce back out of the crap better than most adults do."

"That still don't make it right. It's not their shit. It's mine. I'm responsible. It's not their problem."

Dougie looked at his sister, and Maxine saw that her brother was struggling to keep his emotions in check.

The following morning Dougie waited on his boat, a Cape Islander called the Judy G, as it moved gently alongside the Government wharf, tire buoys squeaking against the gunwales. It was overcast; the clouds hung low and threatened rain. He could see his home from the wheelhouse and he quietly hoped that his children would come over before the school bus picked them up. It was getting on, the bus would arrive soon.

He watched them leave the house and walk to the end of the drive. Part of him wanted to call out.

Kyle, his 14-year-old son, looked over toward the wharf. His daughter Sandy, the elder, did not. The bus arrived on time, then departed. He watched it slowly drive by, searching the windows for the faces of his children. He didn't see them. His heart became heavy and he felt sick.

When he glanced back toward the house, Kyle was still standing at the end of the driveway.

Dougie moved out of the wheelhouse and up to the prow. He stretched out a hand, waved. His son saw him and started walking toward the wharf. The boy's body was hunched and his eyes stayed on the ground.

As Dougie watched him approach, he wondered how this was going to play out with Joan. The last thing they needed was a civil war where the children were stuck in a foxhole in no man's land.

Kyle looked uncomfortable as he made his way along the wharf to his father's boat. He stopped short of the prow and stared. Crude graffiti painted in pink under the name of the boat read: "Faghot's boat." Kyle raised an eyebrow.

"That's original," he said.

Dougie nodded and smiled. "Yup. Wouldn't expect anythin' less round here...How're youse doin', Kyle?"

The boy shrugged and looked out toward Horse Island. "Okay, guess. You?"

"Oh, day's still young. Might get better. Thanks for droppin' by. Appreciate it."

He smiled, and his son grinned, albeit briefly. The boy kicked a piece of stone off the wharf into the water and watched it sink. "Will you be comin' back home, dad?"

"That's not up to me, Kyle. Your mom...Don't think for one minute that I don't want to be back home with youse and your sister. Tell Sandy that. She needs to know, whatever happens between your mom an' me...I love youse both, I always will. Tell your sister that."

"Uh-huh, I will. You're not gay, are you, dad?"

"No, son, I'm not gay."

"Mom said she caught you dressed up, in her clothes. Dancin'...wearin' makeup..." He shrugged, shuffled, and could not look his father in the eye.

"It's called crossdressing, Kyle. Look at me, son..."

Kyle stared at his father, and Dougie could see the boy was close to tears.

"It's not about being gay. Your mom gets mixed up. it's not her fault, it's a common prejudice, or it's a dumb mistake, whatever. Some crossdressers, it's true, are that way inclined, but that's not me, Kyle...and whether she wishes to believe it or not, I still love your mom very much."

The boy stared at his father, his eyes searching, trying to understand. He nodded. "It's kinda funny, dad."

"What is?"

"I was thinkin' about it just before, at breakfast. I mean, here's you, dressin' up like a woman, in private, whatever, doin' your thing, your secret; well, not anymore, but you know what I'm saying. An' there's mom this mornin', like always, she's putting on her Corrections uniform, lookin' all mean an' butch in blue with that new crew cut she's got goin', an' honest to God, I swear, she looks like a guy, 'cept for the jugs...Shouldn't have said that. Didn't mean to be disrespectful to mom, just...I'm sorry."

Kyle dumped his backpack on the concrete and looked out to sea.

Dougie stepped off the boat onto the wharf, he put his arm around the boy's shoulders. He wished he had the words to make things better, to make everything clearer. But he didn't.

A few hours later, Kyle was scraping the crude pink graffiti off his father's boat. The smell of cigarette smoke reached him before a shadow covered what it was he was doing.

Looking over his shoulder, he saw the grinning troll, the pallid features of Larry Dauphinee, with his nicotine-stained teeth and bat-like ears, a greasy Maple Leafs ball cap pressed down hard on his scalp, and eyes that resembled a ferret's.

"Looks like someone added a new name to yer father's boat, eh?"

"Yup. Some asshole...Any ideas, Larry?"

Larry laughed. He looked around, making sure nobody was watching, then leaned in closer to Kyle. "Could be that someone knows sumpthin' youse don't."

Kyle looked at Larry with barely concealed contempt. "You wanna tell my dad that?"

Larry sniggered, didn't reply, turned on his heel and walked away. Kyle watched him open the battered grey door that led upstairs to the wharf office. The boy spat into the water.

Dougie came out of his house with sandwiches and a thermos. The decapitated garden gnome, still cheerily smiling, stared up at him as he walked over the front lawn back toward the wharf.

As he passed Larry's beige Datsun, something caught his eye in the driver's half-open window. He paused. Sitting on the passenger seat was a gallon can of paint, and a brush daubed in pink lay beside it on some newspaper.

Kyle looked up as his father approached. He was hanging out for a cup of coffee. Dougie put the thermos and sandwiches on the boat.

"Seen Larry Dauphinee about?"

"Yeah. That asshole went in there." Kyle nodded toward the office building.

Dougie looked at his son, smiled. He grabbed a ragged-looking mop from the wheelhouse, then stepped back on to the wharf. "Coffee's in the thermos. Back in a bit, son."

"Okay." Kyle stared at his father as he walked back down the wharf, mop in hand.

Joan Hennigar was on her way home from work. She had to gear down her truck as she approached the Government wharf, slowing to a stop.

A large group of fishermen were standing beside a bright pink car. Even the windscreen was painted pink. Most of them were laughing loudly and poking fun at Larry Dauphinee, who was moving around like an agitated rat, with a scrubbing brush in one hand, a bucket in the other, and a stream of invective coursing from his lips that would've made a clam blush.

He moved from hood to trunk, foot to foot, effing and blinding, his face getting redder with rage by the second.

Joan laughed at him, too. She looked toward where her husband's boat was moored. Dougie was standing on the prow staring at her.

He raised a hand, a gentle wave.

13: The woods

Merle Nauss looked up at her husband as he buckled his surplus Sam Browne around his heavy khaki flak jacket. She knew by the look on his weather-beaten face that the question she'd just asked was pointless.

He drained his coffee and then pulled on his plaid hunting cap, glanced out of the window for no particular reason, avoiding her eyes.

"Not as if they need you, Bob. You know that. Got 'nough men out there looking, young men."

The word 'young' bit into him like a deer fly. Bob had turned 68 in August.

"An' none that know them woods like I do, 'cept maybes Cliff. Chances are that new trooper ain't goin' to be listenin' to him. Strikes me as the arrogant type, swaggerin' 'bout like a goddamn mucky-muck."

She frowned at his cussing.

Bob picked up his 30/30 hunting rifle, felt his pockets for the cartridges he knew were there. He'd checked twice already.

"Radio said they were callin' for snow t'night."

"Yup. All the more reason to go," he said.

~

Little Jimmy Ward went missing the afternoon of the day before. The boy was last seen near the old logging road back of St. Cuthbert's Anglican church, so Gerald Sheppard had said.

Clifford Jollymore cocked his head like a border collie when he saw Bob Nauss' truck pull into the hastily-put-together base camp outside the church on the edge of the woods. The two men exchanged nods.

"Nothin' yet?"

"Nope."

Bob grunted. "Figured you'd be out there with 'Dudley Do-Right'."

"Figured wrong." Cliff spat, then took out a cigarette and lit up, his watery pale blue eyes scanning all the assembled trucks, the police prowlers, Laurie's chip wagon, the media circus vans with their brash logos and satellite dishes.

"Gerald here?" Bob asked.

Cliff shook his head, looked away. "Was here yesterday, stayed most'a the night, too."

"You slept yet?"

Cliff looked at Bob as if he just asked a stupid question.

Bob smiled. "What you doin' hangin' 'round here for, anyways?"

"Funny, but thought youse were retired. Actin' like you're still wearin' that damn badge, you old coot."

"Old habits, Cliff. You oughta know that."

"Yeah, well, youse could say I have no intention of followin' fools. Man out there knows shit from candy. Better off here."

He spat some tobacco, a tightness spreading across his brow. Bob sensed something was troubling Cliff, but he knew the man well enough not to prod too hard. Clifford Jollimore was known for his prickly nature.

"Heard the kid had an argument with his mother. That right?"

Cliff nodded. "Yeah, stoopid little...all over a fuckin' dawg. Can you believe that?"

Bob raised an eyebrow as Cliff continued. "Wanted one for Christmas. Mom says no. He runs off in a huff. Now the little bastard's lost. I don't know, Jeezus...Kids."

Cliff slapped the hood of Bob's Dodge. There was a silence between them, broken only by the radio chatter that echoed across the car park from a prowler.

"You find anythin' unusual out there, Cliff?"

"You knows I did, else youse wouldn't be askin'. Boy's got feathers strapped to his feet, he don't like leavin' tracks. Didn't find squat. That's what's unusual."

Bob felt a tingle of alarm crawl up his spine. Prince Rupert...He knew something was wrong.

"Jest tire tracks, nothin' else," Cliff said.

"You tell that to Mister Know-it-all?"

"Course I fuckin' did, an' I may as well have been pissin' into the wind, all the good it did me. Ignorant sonofabitch."

"Kid's not out there, eh?"

Cliff flicked his cigarette butt into a puddle, shook his head. "If I was a bettin' man, I'd say them eejits are out lookin' for a ghost."

Bob stared into the woods. Then he started up his truck.

~

Twenty-three years before, a younger Bob Nauss was in charge of a massive police and volunteer ground search in rugged bush north of Prince Rupert, British Columbia, where he was stationed. A little boy, Michael Rogers, had strayed away from his family's camp site and gotten lost. After a five-day sweep of the area, they had found the boy. But it was too late.

Bob had carried Michael Rogers' body back to the base camp, wrapped in his old Nova Scotian tartan blanket that he kept in his bed roll. The child had died of exposure. It was the saddest day in his whole career as a Mountie.

He would often dream about those five days, reliving every step he took through the dense pine forests, every rock and stream he had crossed, every bear he had sighted, wondering if it was a killer, every order he had given the men under his command, every hour that had passed and the hours he never slept.

Worst of all was recalling the hope of finding the boy alive in 24 hours, the belief that he could because he was a fine hunter and a decent tracker. But as each day ended he had watched the light flicker across tired men's faces around the campfires. The mocking calls of the coyotes forever reminded them that the night was not for men. Hope had sunk into hopelessness as weary bodies lay in sleeping bags, unable to rest. And then there was Rollie, always staring, those big brown wounded eyes that never allowed him to forget.

Bob Nauss thought about all of this as he drove in the general direction of Gerald Sheppard's small farm, glancing in the rear vision mirror to see if Clifford Jollimore was following. He was.

Gerald Sheppard's Chevy van was parked beside the house. Bob turned off his engine and coasted in neutral, the gravel drive silently crunching under the weight of the Dodge tires until he crawled to a halt just behind the Chev.

He watched Cliff park his truck on the road at the top of the drive, half-hidden behind a stand of poplars and maples.

Bob got out of the truck as silently as he'd coasted in. He didn't slam the door; he gently clicked it closed. Walking up the blind side of the house, he took in the curtained windows that faced out toward the dilapidated red barn perched on a slight rise. It had once been a fine farm, but now it looked like crap. Two sides of the house needed re-shingling, the roof had a definite sag over the porch, the lead flushing around the chimney looked loose and battered. *Sad to see a nice old place like this go to the dogs*, he thought as he walked quietly toward the back door.

It crossed his mind that Gerald might be sleeping. By all accounts he'd had a busy night, but Bob doubted it, and he couldn't work out why he felt that.

Somewhere he heard the faint sound of a radio tuned in to some country and western. He listened as the wind played tricks with direction. The sound was coming from the barn. He gripped the hunting rifle and felt his palms were sweaty. He tried to feel nonchalant, but his heart rate had already increased and sweat was forming under the brim of his cap.

He glanced back toward the road. Cliff was now silently stationed beside his truck. They shared a look, then Bob indicated toward the barn. Cliff nodded.

Gerald Sheppard was also sweating, struggling to fit a large wooden door onto the cattle stall at the far end of the barn. His angry red bald patch stuck out between tufts of ginger hair as he heaved the door into place. He didn't hear Bob Nauss come in.

Bob glanced over the rusty 1950s Massey Ferguson tractor, the work bench where tools lay in no particular order, the small radio playing an Emmylou Harris song, a couple of old china cups standing next to a thermos, a shotgun leaning against the wall. A roll of duct tape lay on greasy floorboards not far from where Gerald was working.

Bob was standing not ten feet away when Gerald turned around abruptly. "Mornin' Gerald, workin' hard, eh?"

~

Cliff had lit himself a cigarette, pulled his collar up to the wind. His own rifle, a lever-action Winchester that his grandfather had given him when he was a teen, was propped in the crook of his left arm, the barrel pointed toward the earth. He remembered this farm when cattle were the going concern, but that was over 30 years ago. Gerald Sheppard had moved in ten years back and had never done anything with the land. Cliff thought that was a crying shame.

The gunshot from the barn thundered across the landscape. Cliff instinctively dropped to a crouching position and levelled his Winchester toward the barn doors, his body shielded by the tail end of Gerald's van. His heart was beating fast as he looked down the barrel of the rifle, the sight wavering before him. A good minute passed before he saw Bob standing in the frame of the barn doors, holding up his left hand like a tired man.

He yelled, "Better call an ambulance, Cliff! Get the Mounties whilst you're at it."

Cliff put up his rifle, nodded, then made his way into Gerald's house.

From near the kitchen window where the wall phone was, he watched Bob come out of the barn cradling the small boy, Jimmy Ward.

Cliff kept his eyes on Bob, who appeared to be talking very gently to the boy, holding him close to his burly chest as he walked like a man carrying the most precious cargo in the world.

"Yeah, that's right, there's been a shootin'."

Jimmy Ward was sobbing into khaki, his half-naked little body convulsing to the point where his ribs looked as if they were about to break out of his pale skin.

Cliff muttered, "Sweet Jeezus..." He felt his eyes well up in anger and pity. He quietly hoped for a corpse to be carried out from this run-down shithole of a farm.

~

"I just want to know, off the record, Bob, cop to cop, if you had to shoot Mister Sheppard? I mean, by what you've said in your statement, you had the drop on him, right?"

Bob stared into the prying eyes of Sgt. Dale Stephens, and he knew he'd never take to the man, even if he was wearing the same uniform he himself wore for over 40 years. "Man's still breathin', ain't he? Guess my eyesight's not what it used to be."

Stephens half-frowned and half-smirked.

"He went for his shotgun, gave me no alternative. Why I aimed low, it was a lucky shot."

Stephens butted in. "In the testicles?"

Bob shrugged. "I fired low, went for his legs. All happened pretty quickly."

Dale Stephens nodded, his vacant brown eyes still searching. "Wish you'd spoken to me before you followed your hunch, Bob. Would've appreciated that, one ex-Mountie to..." He held up his right hand in a gesture as if to finish the sentence.

"You were miles back'a the woods. Besides, I listened to what Cliff Jollimore had to say. Guess you could say I smelled a rat. Boy's life was at stake. No time for...bureaucracy."

Stephens' thin black moustache twitched. "We prefer to call it channels of communication, Bob."

Bob smiled. "Still talkin' that departmental manure, are they? Yeah, I know that one all right. I was up in Prince Rupert when a little boy went missin', that was over 23 years ago. Lost in the woods. First Nations fella, Rollie Proudfoot of the Niska. He was a little like Cliff Jollimore is to these parts. Good tracker, the very best. He told me back then where I might find that boy, but I...well, let's just say, cop to cop, I'd just got my stripes, and I thought I was the main man, that I knew everything. I'll tell you somethin' for nothin': if I'd bothered to respect Rollie Proudfoot, to listen to him, I wouldn't have been carrying a dead child back five days later... I live with that shame."

Stephens tapped a pencil on some paperwork. "Well, Mister Sheppard'll live. Lost a lot of blood..."

Bob stared hard at Stephens. "Then he got off lightly. That sonofabitch murdered a childhood."

Stephens got up from behind his desk and glanced out the window where he could see the media vans and reporters waiting. He was thinking about the statement he'd make. He wanted to make a good impression with his superiors. "Bob, I have to ask...You do have a license for your firearm?"

Bob gave Stephens a look of disdain. He was glad he was retired. Pencil pushers in uniform always made him feel sick to his stomach.

~

Bob lay beside Merle and listened to the sound of the poplars rustling in the wind. If it didn't snow tonight the lawn would be covered in a faded gold carpet come the morning. As he listened to every creak and groan in the house it helped take his mind off what he had seen in that cow stall. And yet the frightened face of the boy would not leave him.

It had taken every ounce of morality in his system not to put a bullet between Gerald Sheppard's eyes, and he'd felt a macabre sense of relief when Sheppard had foolishly grabbed for the shotgun. Still, he could have fired a warning shot, he could have put one into that asshole's kneecap. He knew he was a good enough shot to have done that.

But he hadn't lied to Stephens. He did fire low. Reaction, instinct, the hunter's edge...Again, the boy's frightened tear-stained face stared back at him. He'd never seen anything so distraught, helpless, alone. He tried to close his eyes, block the image out, but it was no good.

He sat up in bed, thought about making a cup of hot chocolate, or maybe he needed a glass of rum. God knows he needed something...*Help me, Jesus...Help me, please...I don't want to remember...I want to forget...Please God, help me...*

Merle's small gentle hand reached out and took him by the elbow. "I'm so proud of you," she said.

He looked at his wife, then he started to sob, a deep guttural whine that sounded like a wild animal confined to the smallest of spaces.

She held him for over an hour.

14: The course

Gracie Cheeseman believed that her husband went off the rails the night that Bundle died. Though she was at a loss to explain why, convinced as she was that he'd never really liked the cat. Why would the cat's death send an elderly man like Barney Cheeseman over the edge? She did not know. And neither did their few remaining friends in the dwindling St. James' Anglican Church congregation, fellow members of the bowling club, and her best friend Clementine, the Bridgetown librarian.

Most were genuinely shocked by Barney's bizarre criminal behaviour. Gossip reigned as gossip does, but remained as vacuous as a Facebook conversation. The truth was that nobody really knew anything.

One month and one week before his 77th birthday, Barney was sitting in his small study next to the bathroom. He was trying to read but could not concentrate. Bundle's intermittent cries were distracting and distressing him. Barney knew that the little tabby was dying, and he figured that tonight was going to be her last stand.

He put the Graham Greene novel down, took off his spectacles and pinched the bridge of his nose, then slowly stood up, making sure not to put his back out. He walked quietly into the bathroom to look in on the emaciated cat lying in her box behind the bathtub.

She hadn't moved from the last time he'd looked. She lay flat, breathing heavily, and her eyes remained glassy, vacant. He crouched for a closer look. His right knee cracked, and he grimaced.

He thought of his father, a man who would not have given a second thought about putting a sick cat in a sack with a brick in the river: "Putting it out of its misery," he'd have said. But Barney could not do that.

A sound he'd heard before, and not so long ago, started to peal from the cat.

The death-rattle. He stood up, turned away and stared out of the small bathroom window that looked out upon the golf course. Bundle rattled on for a few minutes more, then a sad kind of high-pitched sigh ended it.

Barney felt his eyes moisten, but he kept his gaze on the 9th hole, where a limp red flag clutched at its pole in the moonlight. "Godspeed, cat," he whispered.

Minutes later he bent down and reached out, touching the cat's fur. Her little body was still warm, but her eyes were without light. The cat that had always lived in their bathroom, ever since Gracie had found it half-dead on Granville Street some years back, was gone.

He walked out of the bathroom, through his study, down the stairs to the kitchen, then into the laundry. On the middle shelf he found a box of latex gloves.

Gracie was in bed reading when Barney's presence made her look up. He stood in the doorway, not venturing over the threshold.

"Cat's dead," he said.

She put her book down and stared at her husband, whose face was half-hidden in shadow, unable to read him.

"I'll bury her near the lilacs in the morning. It was quick...she didn't linger." His voice sounded different. Slightly choked.

"Oh, dear. I should have stayed up with her, Barney. I thought she'd see the morning..."

"Makes no difference now. Besides, you said your goodbyes, so don't go all catholic on me. Just a cat."

He left the shadows of the doorway and she heard him go into the bathroom and run a tap.

"It was our cat, Barney! Our cat!" She didn't really believe he could be so hardhearted. That wasn't him. No, he was being flippant because that's how he dealt with unhappiness, with death.

~

At breakfast they exchanged few words. It was the routine. Gracie ate her Weetabix cereal while reading *The Chronicle-Herald*; Barney drank his coffee and listened to the local breakfast program on CBC radio.

The discussion today centred around an infestation of rats in downtown Halifax. He guffawed at the host's concerns about the possibility of disease being spread in the downtown core, then switched the radio off.

Gracie folded the paper and sighed. "No news in the paper today. Very slim."

"Yup. Nothin' interestin' on the radio either. Cat's in the laundry, if you want a final look before..." He left the sentence hanging and stared out of the window.

"Will you make a little cross for her?"

Barney nodded. "Already have. Made it a few days back."

She followed her husband into the laundry. A small black and white Adidas shoe box sat on top of the washing machine. He took the lid off the box. The cat rested among what looked like scrunched-up balls of tissue paper.

Gracie stared at the tabby. She ran her fingers over the little body, then started to cry. He put his large gnarled hands on her shoulders and held her close to him. He could smell the tea tree shampoo she used.

~

As he planted the shovel into the earth, he heard the first golf cart of the day approach the 9th green. He watched quietly from under the lilac trees as two obese men dressed in brightly coloured v-neck sweaters, one yellow, the other fuchsia, lumbered out of their cart and started searching for their balls. Mr. Fuchsia found his in the bunker and cursed at the lie. Mr. Yellow, who was also wearing an alarmingly tight pair of tartan shorts, found his ball in the rough just off the green.

Daniel Lillford

As Barney dug the small grave for the cat, he recalled a gentler era when the golf course didn't have carts, when young boys made a few dollars caddying for the rich, when it used to be called a walking game and, above all, a gentleman's game. His father had been the head groundskeeper throughout the 1930s and into the Korean War years.

As a boy, Barney used to sit on the tractor with his father, who would let him steer the Massey-Ferguson down the big fairways, cutting the grass with the gang-mowers clanking behind. After school he'd wade into the water traps collecting golf balls in a net to resell at the clubhouse for pocket money, money he diligently saved that would one day help pay for his first car, a '54 Olds.

The small shoe box went snugly into the hole he had dug beneath the lilacs. He heaped earth upon it. When he was done, a small pyramid of dirt lay at his feet. He patted the dirt down with the shovel, then walked off toward the shed.

He was about to open the old red door when a golf ball flew past his head and smashed into the shingles, chipping paint off the building, and bounced onto the lawn. Some clown had overshot their fairway drive. Not an unusual occurrence on this hole, a par three, which had deceived many a professional and legions of rank amateurs.

Barney picked up the ball, a Callaway, and pocketed it.

A small wooden cross lay on his workbench among shavings and tools. In the middle of the cross he'd carved the cat's name, 'Bundle'.

He picked up some sandpaper and took the cross off the bench. The maple wood felt smooth to his touch, but he gave it a gentle sand while thinking about the stain he'd use. Something red, he thought.

Old, unvarnished persimmon drivers' heads sat in a line like a collection of Peterson pipes, waiting for their hickory shafts. His father's work, from another age, when his father made his own wooden drivers during the long winter months for his small boutique mail-order business with golfers who lived in the States. He remembered helping his father most winter nights, sanding and sanding. Always sanding.

Now he sat in what used to be his father's chair, and the apple box beside the bench was where he'd sat as a boy. The old valve radio, long dead now, waited on a shelf above the bench, and he recalled the warmth of its light, always a yellow hue, and the hum it made before it came on. It had kept them company with Don Messer's CBC show when the snow was three feet deep outside the shed door, and the small wood stove had kept them warm.

His father never spoke much when he was working, but he smiled a lot. Barney could still see the old man's crinkly blue eyes, called 'dancing eyes' by family and friends...Yup, another age.

He thought about how everything was made of steel now, from golf drivers to baseball bats. All cold, unwelcoming to the touch. He wondered about the world he lived in, the hardness he felt around him, the changing manufacturing mores.

An old Gil Elvgrin calendar from 1957 still hung above the unvarnished drivers, faded and crumbling away at the edges. Miss June. Yesteryear's model. Beautiful. Gone.

He finished sanding the cross and, after giving it a once-over, decided it was ready for staining. Remembering the golf ball in his pocket, he took it out and tossed it into a four-gallon bucket that was already half-full of lost balls.

As he stepped outside he heard the sound of a tractor. The head groundskeeper, Donald Hamilton, a man he did not like, parked the big blue Holland tractor most mornings on a blind rise where the trees met the rough. There he would take a break, sometimes a nap, for about 40 minutes. Then he'd wake up just in time for lunch.

Barney had watched 'old Mudguts', as he referred to Hamilton, and his sly ways for many years. He knew that his small crew of men did all the real work; Hamilton merely coasted on their sweat and effort, scooping up the credit from the owners in the process. Barney had tried to tell the new owners a few hard facts, being the elder retired groundskeeper living almost on the course as he did, but they appeared uninterested, dismissive. It was clear to Barney that they thought that the sun shone out of Donald Hamilton's ass.

'Old Mudguts' had certainly pulled the wool over their eyes. Not that Barney cared, but he hated seeing people duped by lazy scoundrels like Hamilton. *More fools them*, he thought. *Let Hamilton bleed you, because I sure as hell know he will.*

They say you can tell a helluva lot about a business, about the boss, by the staff turnover rate. Since Donald Hamilton had wrangled the job as head groundskeeper some ten years back, Barney had counted 23 different groundsmen under his charge who had moved on after the golfing season was over for another year. In his day, and in his father's time, the small crews remained the same groups of men year in, year out. They became fixtures at the course, seasonal friends to the regulars.

As Barney chewed on a tuna sandwich, he stared out the kitchen window at the half-hidden tractor, and the outlined lump of Hamilton asleep at the wheel. He spoke his mind: "Cream always rises to the top...so do turds."

~

Perhaps it was the sacrilege at the cat's grave later that week that finally tipped the balance...Gracie could never be certain. She had come home from working at the St. James ACW salad plate lunch-eon to find Barney standing by the lilac trees, beside himself in fury. His face was the colour of beetroot, blotched, and he could hardly contain the spittle that was dribbling from the corners of his mouth. His fists were clenched and his whole body was as rigid as a steel pole.

Gracie approached him quickly with a sense of growing alarm. She'd never seen him like this before. She touched his arm. "Barney, what, what's wrong? What is it?"

Barney made noises, but no words formed. He pointed at the cat's grave.

The mound of earth had been trampled over. Clear spike marks from a pair of golf shoes marked the earth where a deep weight had stood and hacked out a golf ball from below the lilacs. Some branches were bent in on themselves, as if they'd been pushed that way. The small wooden cross was broken and lying lopsided against the tree; placed there like a guilty afterthought.

It wasn't uncommon for golf balls to fly into the Cheesemans' back garden, but in all their years of living beside the course, no golfer had ever disrespected their private property by playing a shot from the garden to get back onto the green. Gracie was at a loss for words. It was like an ancient law had been violated.

She recalled a similar feeling when she'd lived in the city while studying to be a nurse, and had come back to her apartment one night to find it had been burgled. She felt that sick feeling again now, as she clutched at Barney's arm.

~

A Bard owl hooted. Gracie looked out into the garden, to the shed, and saw that the light was still burning strong. Barney was working on the new cross for the cat's grave.

She'd thought about asking him if he wanted a cup of hot chocolate, but decided against it. He was being uncommunicative, and she knew her husband well enough by now to just let him alone.

She made her hot drink and went upstairs to bed.

Barney stared at the new cross. He wasn't happy with it, and he knew why. He'd worked quickly, in anger, in haste, to right a wrong. And all he had accomplished was a second-rate job. His father would have looked at him in that way of his, and he would know by the look in his eyes that he was disappointed...as disappointed as Barney was with himself right now.

He threw the mallet across the room. "Shit...! Shit!" He stabbed the chisel into the cross and left it there.

~

It was a muggy night. The air was heavy, pregnant with the perfumes of summer.

Barney decided to go for a walk around the course, to help

drown out those voices inside his head. Walking the course was something he had done all his life, in all seasons; walking had always managed to clear the cobwebs away.

He made his way along the fairway and then cut through a stand of pines alongside the 7th tee. An owl hooted close by; its call was answered from further afield.

The gravel track that led to the maintenance sheds took him through an open steel gate. He was surprised it wasn't locked.

As he moved closer toward the main shed, intending to cut across the fairway that led to the 10th green, a dim light spilling from the workshop window stopped him in his tracks. It was after 10 pm. Nobody should be around here now.

Curious, he decided to investigate. From the safety of the shadows, looking through the workshop window, he saw Donald Hamilton filling up gas cans out of the 44-gallon shop drum. Hamilton then put the gas cans in the back of his truck, which was parked alongside the tractors and the greens lawnmowers. Hamilton was helping himself to his employer's gasoline.

"You lowdown dirty bastard," Barney muttered. He wished he had a camera.

He watched Hamilton open the doors quietly, then drive his truck out into the yard without turning on the headlights. Hamilton lumbered out of the truck, locked up the shed, then placed the key where it was always kept, under a rock near the door. Then he got back into his truck and quietly drove away.

He won't put his lights on until he closes the gate, Barney thought, *to keep those fools up at the big house from noticing anything suspicious.*

He held the shed key in his hand, a key to a padlock that hadn't been changed in over 30 years. He clicked open the lock and stood in the doorway of the shop.

The silhouettes of machinery, the smell of cut grass, gasoline, oil, mingled with greens chemicals and paint thinners. Quite the cocktail, one that still brought a smile to his face. There would be paint brushes resting in thinner in the large, stained industrial sink, cleaning out the green enamel paint used for the gates around the course.

He walked through the past, his past. The small office, a partition really, was quite bare. Gone were all the black and white photographs that he used to have on the walls.

Paperwork lay on the oak desk, receipts stabbed on a spike, a telephone, scribble pad.

Hamilton's coveralls hung from a hook near an army-green metal filing cabinet.

A buxom young woman lying on the hood of a motor car stared temptingly at him from a calendar. Barney grimaced at the tattoos covering her arms.

The old Massey-Ferguson was still there. That made him smile. He ran a hand over the faded and chipped red mudguard. The other equipment was relatively new, from the bright orange Kubota greens mowers to the big blue Holland tractor that towered over all. That was the one Hamilton used exclusively. *An arrogant-looking machine,* he thought. *Imperious.*

~

When the RCMP arrived at the golf course the following morning, there was a show of universal head-scratching. The Cooks, the new owners, were in a state of shock. Mr Cook was reported to have taken to his bed, heavily sedated.

Some vandal had driven the big blue tractor on quite the spree the night before. All the golf carts had been flattened, driven over. Complete write-offs. The greens on 7, 9, 10, 12, 13, 15 and 18 were ruined. Massive ruts criss-crossed each green's surface.

The tractor was half-submerged in the water trap on the 16th fairway.

Constable Laval stared at the tractor. "Whoever did this sure hates golf...Any ideas, Mr. Hamilton?"

Hamilton glanced briefly into the dark eyes of the police officer. He shook his head. "Kids, I expect. Goddamn vandals, I know that! Whole season's ruined. Ruined!"

Constable Laval consulted her map of the course, and the rough route of the tractor. "Kids, eh? Well, if they were kids, they knew this course very well."

She pointed out where the tractor had come from, where it went, how each green had been approached and wrecked, and then how the tractor had gone by the fastest route to the next green, often bypassing the fairways. "There was no luck involved here. Whoever did this knew exactly what they were doing. And the maintenance shed was unlocked, so someone knew where to find the key to get at the tractor. Any ex-employees come to mind who might hold a grudge, Mr. Hamilton?"

Hamilton tried to laugh off her question, but he felt perspiration form on his temples. His neck started to go red. Ex-employees... where would he start? He remembered some who wouldn't think twice about punching him in the nose, given the opportunity.

The police officer did not drop her gaze. She was used to questioning the guilty, and there was something about Donald Hamilton that irked her, and she did not trust him. His furtive glances creeped her out.

"Perhaps we should start by going through the records of the past employees, eh?"

~

Later that morning, Gracie was nervously watching a police officer inspecting the damage on the 9th green. Constable Laval looked up, smiled, waved, and walked toward her.

"He...he's in the shed..."

The policewoman looked quizzically.

"My husband, Barney. In the shed." She pointed, a little offhandedly.

"Do you think I should speak to your husband, Mrs...?"

Gracie nodded, she reached for a handkerchief from her apron, dabbed at her eyes. "Mrs. Cheeseman. I'm Mrs. Grace Cheeseman. This way, officer."

Gracie's birdlike frame moved quickly away from the lilac trees.

"Mrs. Cheeseman, do you know anything about what happened

on the golf course last night?"

Gracie glanced at the constable. "It's, it's best you talk to my husband, officer. You see, he's not, not been himself since the cat died. I don't know what's happened to him."

Constable Laval wasn't quite sure if she'd heard right, but the sight of this frail old lady, obviously upset, left her hanging between knocking on the shed door and giving the old lady a hug.

The faint sound of music came from within the shed. She thumped on the door. "Mr. Cheeseman, it's the police!"

A voice called from inside, "Door's unlocked, come in!"

The policewoman instinctively placed her right hand on her holster as she lifted the latch on the door and opened it.

Barney Cheeseman was standing beside the wood stove. He was wearing golfing attire from the late 1930s: forest Tweeds, plus fours, Argyle socks and two-tone leather shoes. They had once been his father's clothes. The RCMP officer, from Quebec, thought he looked like an elderly version of Tin-Tin.

The music she had heard was coming from a small tape recorder. Julie London was singing about a cottage for sale. Barney turned the tape off.

"Ah, Mr. Cheeseman, I just want to ask—"

"I did it. I'm your man."

Constable Laval stared, mildly intrigued.

Gracie stood in the doorway, her face red from crying. "Oh, Barney..."

"I see. Could you tell me exactly what it is you have done, Mr. Cheeseman?"

"Certainly. I destroyed half the greens on the course, and I flattened those lousy, rhino-butt-carryin' golf carts. Oh, and sent that lazy, thievin' sonofabitch's big tractor into the water trap on the 16th. I think that about covers it."

"Okay...Would you care to, to tell me why you did it?"

Barney shrugged, glanced at Gracie. He moved toward the workbench and picked up some sandpaper. A small wooden cross lay on the bench, the name 'Bundle' carved out in the middle. He gently sanded the edges.

Daniel Lillford

When he spoke, it was in a quiet and measured tone. "It used to be a walkin' game, you know. A gentleman's game...Ladies', too. That was a long time ago. Nowadays it's populated by the fat men. Slobs in carts. Rushin' all over the place like lunatics, an' seein' nothin' in the process. You can't see the beauty of the landscape like that. I doubt they'd even notice a cardinal singin', or the chickadees chirrupin', darting between the trees as the sun starts to rise over the putting greens. Such a wonderful time of day... No, sir, not them. No style. Just loud. Too goddamn lazy to walk, too fat to exercise. Too rich to care. The course is nothin' but a blur, an exercise in killing time, a seasonal status symbol. There is no love of the world, what we created here, what my father helped create... No love of the game neither, not really, not as it was meant to be played. Blind ignorance never did appreciate truth nor beauty."

He stopped sanding, put the cross down, then looked at a black and white photograph on the shelf where the old valve radio was. The photograph depicted a crew of groundsmen from the 1930s, all dressed in shirts, ties, vests, cloth caps and plus fours. They were smiling, happy.

"I guess it's just a different world...And I guess I hate it."

Constable Laval looked at the cross. "Who was Bundle?"

Tears slid gently down Barney Cheeseman's face. "The cat. She used to live in the bathroom..."

Gracie made her way to stand by her husband. She rested her head on his shoulder.

Constable Laval took a good look around the shed and considered the old-world charm of Mr. Barney Cheeseman. This morning, this summer's morning, she wished she wasn't a cop.

15: Red carnations

Shirley Hirtle found her husband of 42 years lying face-down in chicken shit and wood shavings. He still held a basket of eggs in his hand; remarkably none were broken. She noticed he wasn't wearing his wedding ring.

His favourite chicken, a big black Osterloh called Queenie, was perched on his orange tuque, pecking at his head as if trying to wake him up.

The last thing Albert Hirtle had said to his wife that morning was, "Goin' out to collect the eggs."

It could just as easily have been yesterday morning, or the day before that, or last month, even last year. She looked at his body and felt numb, but no wave of grief sent her insides into paroxysms. Shirley felt a sense of relief, though she did not know why.

At the funeral service the Reverend Folger was talking about Albert, what little he knew about the man, to a large congregation at St. Mark's. Shirley wasn't listening, she wasn't really paying much attention to anything. Like the last few days, it was all a bit grey and fogbound, and she was hoping it would finish quickly. She held her cream lace handkerchief close to her small mouth and the black veil put half her face in shadow. She was not crying. Her eyes, which protruded slightly, were always watery.

Her son, Robert, held her hand, and her daughter, Evelyn, gently rubbed her mother's back in small arcs. The five grandchildren sat directly behind, all but one looking bored and wanting to be elsewhere. Two were surreptitiously playing games on their iPhones.

"Albert was a good man," Reverend Folger said, "a man respected in this church, this community, and as we know very well here at St. Mark's, a man possessed of a fine baritone voice."

Daniel Lillford

The Reverend glanced toward the St. Mark's choir pews with a grin. A few of the choristers nodded solemnly, some smiled, but Margaret St. Clair stifled a sob and turned away, tears cascading.

As the Reverend Folger continued with more of his well-intentioned generalizations, Shirley Hirtle kept her gaze on Margaret St. Clair. She'd often suspected her husband had something going on with that woman, that American, though she could never prove it.

Albert had always been a terrible flirt. He liked women and they liked him. He had an easy charm about him, not to mention a never-ending supply of off-colour jokes, and it wasn't so unusual for some woman to fall a little in love with the old rascal.

Margaret St. Clair was, for her age, an attractive widow. Tall and gracious, she had an air of nobility about her that Shirley found irksome. Singing in the choir had always been one of Albert's joys in life. For a man who never learnt to read sheet music, never played an instrument, he had a remarkable gift for understanding it. Shirley had never liked it when he praised Margaret's lovely voice, or when he'd started calling her "The Connecticut angel."

When the choir rose to sing Streams of Living Justice, a hymn that Albert had adored, Shirley noticed that Margaret St. Clair wasn't singing at all. She stood in her choir pew, head bowed, weeping.

Shirley smiled. "You silly old bitch," she muttered to herself.

The farm was not the same now that Albert was gone. His beloved chickens, all 56 of them, were a chore she had never realized needed so much attention. Time and her ever-present arthritis were at constant loggerheads with each other.

Also, there were so many things Albert had done around the house that she had taken for granted. Not many men of his generation took care of washing and drying the laundry every week, or vacuuming the sitting room, cleaning the bathroom, washing the dishes, *et cetera*. A pang of guilt would hit her when-ever she felt tired and another chore, a chore Albert had always taken care of, required her attention.

Had she been a nagging wife? She had told him he didn't do enough often enough. She heard herself saying it. It rang in her head like a broken bell. He'd look at her with those wounded eyes of his and walk away, wouldn't communicate for days, unless it was to his damn birds. She didn't want to think about it now, but sleep never comes easy when a conscience feels guilty.

Queenie was ill. Shirley had tried everything she knew to get the hen better; but secretly she wondered if the old girl wasn't just pining away for Albert. He had loved that hen. It was the only one he'd put under his arm and carry about. He even let it wander around the garage when he was working there. No other chicken ever had such special privileges. Shirley had caught him talking to it like it was a child on numerous occasions. He'd even take it out on the tractor with him when he was plowing their few acres. They had been inseparable.

Her children wanted their mother to think seriously about selling the farm. It was too much upkeep for an elderly woman to maintain on her own. Of course, she knew they were right and meant well. It was just a pity that neither of them was interested in farming. That was the younger generation all over, so far as she was concerned.

But it was Albert who had said, all those years ago, "Youse can't make 'em love the life we live. They have to find their own way."

Shirley had always disliked his rational way of looking at the bigger picture. She was the emotional one and he was the exact opposite; and yet, as the years had rolled on by, it was Albert who had become more emotionally attached to things, whereas she became less interested in the past, holding on to her present or her future, whatever that might be.

She recalled a yard sale she'd set up some ten years back, and how Albert had gotten upset when he saw books he'd read to their children in a crate to be sold off. Shirley thought he was behaving irrationally, and she lost her temper with him, calling him an insulting name.

What she didn't know, couldn't know, was that was the day he fell out of love with his wife. He had looked at her, the box of children's books between them, and didn't know who she was any more. He saw a nag, a dried-up, selfish woman he did not recognize, and his heart was dulled, as if black clouds had settled over it. That was, as they say, the straw that broke the camel's back.

He kept the children's books; hid them away in his garage. When the grandchildren came along he'd hoped to be able to read the same old stories all over again. He looked forward to that.

But his own children left Nova Scotia; Robert went to Calgary with his company and his growing family, and his Evelyn now worked for the Federal government in Ottawa. So not only did they leave the old family farm, they left the old province, too.

If they broke his heart, he never let it show. Shirley knew it hit him hard. Not being able to see their grandchildren on a regular basis hurt them both, but she knew it affected him the worst. She still had her part-time job down the road at the Seniors Care Home, but Albert had a lot of time to himself on the farm. His only other outlet was the church choir; regular practice on Thursday mornings, and practice every Sunday before the 11 am service.

What Shirley would never know was that Albert did read those stories he couldn't read to his grandchildren. He read them to his hens when she was out working. Usually on Friday mornings. He'd sit on a bale of straw in the hen house and read to them chapters from *Winnie the Pooh*, *Treasure Island* or something by Dr. Seuss, with Queenie on his lap.

His relationship with Margaret St. Clair started not long after the 'children's books yard sale' incident. He was at choir practice. Margaret's car was at the local garage, could he give her a lift home? Of course he could. It was on his way. The invite to come in for a coffee was perhaps imprudent, but willingly accepted, and he went into her house.

When he came out, two hours later, he felt the happiest he'd felt in years. The guilt would come later. The secret would go with him to the grave, or so he'd thought at the time.

Queenie died. Shirley found her in the cardboard box near the heat vent in the kitchen. She'd brought her inside to keep her away from the other hens. Feeding her rice in milk helped to perk the bird up for a day or two, but then she stopped eating and began to loll. Her neck was floppy and her eyes were half-closed. The will to live seemed to have left her. Shirley knew the end was near, so she let nature take its course.

She burned the carcass in the furnace.

In a phone call from out of the blue, a co-worker at the Senior's home alerted Shirley to Albert's grave in an offhand comment. A full year had passed, and she had not visited his grave since the funeral.

Apparently someone had been leaving bouquets of carnations, beautiful red carnations. Why her co-worker bothered to inform her of this she never asked.

Perhaps it was a blessing, albeit a crude one, that a mink got into the hen house and massacred the entire flock. Shirley was a sound sleeper; she never heard their cries for help. Albert would have, he was a light sleeper.

When she went to feed and water them the next morning she walked into a place of unspeakable carnage. The mink had decapitated most of the birds and had lain them side by side in what seemed like some sort of weird satanic ritual.

Once Shirley had recovered from the shock and cleaned up the mess, the coop stood silent and empty. No more eggs to collect or sell at the gate, no more raking up chicken shit, nor feeding, watering…That was all over. It was the end of an era.

As she stood there in the empty coop, this old converted barn that her husband had doted over, amidst the dust particles, feathers, straw, the smell of death, crap and wood, she felt for the first time ever all alone. She leaned on the rake in the quiet and closed her eyes.

But all she could hear was his voice, talking to his birds. "Shut up, she said, for God's sake, shut up!"

On a visit into town she popped into the local florist. Jenny Saunders greeted her with a look of surprise, but was happy to have a customer midweek in a small country business.

"Red carnations, Jenny: do you have any?"

Jenny knew she didn't, she'd sold all she had the day before. "Not red, Mrs Hirtle. I do have white…"

"Oh, that's a pity. I was hoping for red."

"I'll be getting some more in soon."

"I suppose Mrs St. Clair's been buying up all the red ones again?"

She asked her question in a joking fashion, and Jenny nodded and affirmed what she needed to know. "Yes, she was here yesterday. She usually buys a few bouquets every few weeks"

Shirley smiled as she left the florist shop. *She goes on Tuesdays*, she thought.

It was the dog-days of August. Not much was moving. The graveyard was darkened by its immense canopy of summer foliage, a welcome refuge from the heat. The late morning air was thick to breathe and something sweet and fertile carried itself in on a ghost breeze. Maples and oaks shaded vast tracts of sleeping bones; over two centuries of death in a small country town.

As cemeteries go, it was a pleasant one. Some might even call it quaint. A verdant, mossy world where it would not be so unusual to hear a satyr's pipes, if one had the ear for that sort of thing. Spared the savagery of modernity, with its stark treeless lines of corporatized headstones, the tranquil twisting gravel walkways under ancient bows and limbs were, as they should be in such a place as this, peaceful and calming. It was a quiet sanctuary for thought, for remembrance; a place to talk or sit for a while with one's beloved.

Shirley stared at the withered red carnations on her husband's grave. She was tempted to kick them away from his headstone, but she did not, instead she walked toward a large oak and stood in its shadows.

Within the hour she saw a tall woman enter the graveyard, coming from the old railway trail. She was wearing a bottle-green blouse, a pleated cream skirt, and a battered straw hat. She carried a bouquet of red carnations.

Moving quietly along the pathways that led toward where Albert Hirtle lay, Shirley watched Margaret St. Clair stand in front of his grave. She crossed herself, then she knelt down and removed the withered flowers, replacing them with fresh ones.

Shirley moved out of the shadows, standing no more than eight yards from the other woman.

It was Margaret St. Clair who broke the silence. "Beautiful morning, isn't it Mrs Hirtle?"

Shirley was taken off guard, more so when Margaret rose, a little shakily, and looked her in the eyes. "Al liked red carnations. His favourite flower, so he told me."

Shirley gazed into clear hazel eyes and she saw no malice nor any fear. "He, he always liked flowers," she found herself saying without knowing why, then wishing she'd said nothing.

"Yes, flowers, days like today, a cold beer, singing and chickens…"

Margaret laughed a little. Then she looked back at the gravestone where she'd placed the carnations. "I loved your husband very much. I suspect you already know that."

Her off-hand confession rocked Shirley. It was like a naval exchange between battle cruisers where shells hit water close to the ship and great tubs of grey iron lurch in the waves.

"What a brazen female you are. Of all the…Have you no shame? You took my husband away from me!"

Margaret half-chuckled. "If you believe that, then he was right. Was he right? Are you a terribly selfish woman?"

"How dare you!"

"Talk openly and honestly with you? Really? Please try to act like a grownup. We'll both be lying here sooner rather than later. We have so little time for girlish caprices and twelfth-grade lies, don't you think?"

"All I know is that you are an adulterous woman who turned my husband away from me!"

Margaret St. Clair shook her head. "What an ignorant, foolish woman you are."

Shirley felt her temperature rise. She went to take a step forward but a look of cold steel put her back where she had started.

"Turned him away from what exactly? A sexless, loveless marriage? A cold comfort farm? A nag who was never satisfied? Good God, woman, what the hell was there for him to stay for? But for all that, he did stay, he still came home to you, the damned fool. I never asked him why. Duty probably; fear of the unknown, the threat of change. Men are so weak and indecisive. But you're dead wrong. I never took him away. How on earth could I take away what you had thrown away years ago? If I am an adulteress, then I plead guilty, without remorse. Such an old-fashioned word. I prefer, mistress."

"The other 'old-fashioned' word is whore!"

Margaret St. Clair stared at Shirley, shook her head sadly, then turned to leave. Shirley grabbed Margaret's arm, raising her other spindly hand to strike out.

The two older women stared at one another. Shirley gritted her teeth and spat out her words. "Albert was my husband, you Yankee bitch!"

Margaret smiled at her, then she looked toward the grave. "Yes, you had that honour. Where are your flowers, Mrs Hirtle?"

The two women stared at each other for what felt like a full minute. Slowly, Shirley's grip lessened until her hand limply rested by her side. She started to whimper, her bottom lip fluttering up and down like a tent flap in a breeze. She felt like she was melting as she slowly sank to her knees, a weeping wreck.

Margaret St. Clair looked at her with a mixture of disgust and pity, then turned and walked away without looking back.

16: A better life

John Burton put on his worn rubber boots as he sat beside the wood stove. It was the warmest place in his house. He opened the fire door and rubbed his thin hands together, stretching them out toward the flames. As always, the battery radio was tuned to CBC. Seasonal favourites had been playing for the last half-hour, and John found himself humming along to "God Rest Ye, Merry Gentleman".

For a moment he was transported back to his old school in England, standing in the chapel dressed in a black blazer with red piping, white shirt, tie and grey pants, a small boy in a school choir. He recalled the carols he had to rehearse every Christmastime, and the energetic, if slightly eccentric, choir master, Mr. Challenor, whose ears stuck out and had tufts of hair poking out of them the same colour as his droopy walrus nicotine-stained moustache. When old "Tufty" Challenor was on the podium, baton flailing, his mangy black gown flapping behind him, he bore a striking resemblance to a dishevelled bat suffering from modern dance moves.

And then there were the faces of the choir itself, long-ago-lost boys, forgotten classmates...They were happy days. His father had told him that his school days would be some of the happiest days of his life. He hadn't believed him, not then. What boy would? Fathers only become wise when their sons reach 24.

The radio program host interrupted his thoughts. Those post-war English school days were a long way away from the here and now; another world away from rural Nova Scotia, December 2001, a few days before Christmas.

The snow was thick on the ground, over three feet deep in the drifts. Two days earlier a blizzard had whited out the countryside.

Daniel Lillford

The spruce trees were weighted down, dripping fudge-like icing.

Starlings had congregated on the roof next to the chimney and were making a lot of noise. John counted at least 40 as he moved from the dilapidated barn with a sled full of wood dragging behind him. Apart from the starlings, the world where he lived was very still this morning. He pulled the sled to the front door of his house, parked it and picked up an armful of logs, carrying them up the steps and inside.

The stove top warmed up a dented aluminum kettle. The radio program had moved on from seasonal classics into the realms of the seasonally asinine. As John prepared to make his tea, he couldn't help but become annoyed by the self-centred, shallow comments blurting out from those who had such a lucrative existence at the taxpayers' expense. Half the time he wondered who these people on the radio were really talking to, because it certainly wasn't him or his nearest neighbours. He lost his temper and yelled at some nasally whining idiot complaining about 'colour choices'.

"Who cares about the colour of a fucking computer when you can't afford to buy food? You soulless cretin!"

The front door creaked open, bringing with it an icy draft. He moved to the door and shoved it closed again, placing a block of wood at the base for good measure. Then he switched the radio off, deciding that peace goes best with tea, black tea.

He would have liked a drop of milk in his tea, but as he possessed no fridge there was no milk. In the winter months he often used the snow outside the front door as his fridge. There was no electricity in the house, it had been that way for nearly ten years. There was no telephone either. He couldn't afford one.

As he supped the bitter-tasting tea, he picked up a Christmas card depicting polar bears, his only Christmas card thus far. It was from his neighbours, Trevor and Diana Brixton, who lived a few miles away down the road. Like himself, they were CFAs (come-from-aways) and they shared many of the same immigrant experiences. The Brixtons had two little boys, and Diana was expecting their third child in May.

John had a lot of time for them. They were kind, considerate people. He suspected that it was Trevor who left the "mysterious" food parcels hanging on his front door every now and then. They treated him like their favourite uncle. And that was fine with him. Their little boys, Liam and Joseph, had even started calling him "Uncle John". And that was fine, too.

He looked forward to tomorrow's meal they had invited him to, and also to reading a story or two to the boys, something he always enjoyed. And perhaps, after dinner, they would all sit down to watch a movie together. The thought warmed him.

The loose change from the battered Quality Street tin he'd upended amounted to less than $20. But he knew he had a five dollar note somewhere as he rummaged through his coat where it hung on a peg near the stove. It wasn't in his coat. Perhaps it was in the brown corduroys.

He went upstairs to the bedroom; the cold frigid air immediately hit him once he'd gone up a level. His cords were hanging neatly on the chair at the end of the bed. He found the bill and an unexpected dollar.

The window rattled. Thick, frosted glass looked out onto a snowy landscape, beyond the trees to the grey Atlantic Ocean. How many offers had he had on this property over the years? Prime real estate on the Aspotogan peninsula. They all wanted the land for the view. The house was nothing more than a shack, it wasn't worth anything, he knew that.

But be damned if some grubby developer was getting his hands on this place to wreak havoc on the environment with yet another tasteless architectural monstrosity. It had been his parents' summer cottage, and although it might be falling apart and in dire need of a face-lift, a truckload of insulation and a new chimney, it meant more to him than he could ever explain to anyone; except Diana Brixton.

She understood. Everyone else, including Trevor, had, more or less, told him he was a fool not to sell. It was, as they often reminded him, a seller's market.

What they had failed to understand was his personal attachment to the land itself...his memories. Perhaps they did not want to understand. After all, it was easier to whine about a lack of "colour choices" for some piece of electronic junk than to think of a living, breathing world where real decisions that actually mean something are not always easy to make.

He thought about those fools on the radio and got mad all over again. This time he was angry with himself. *Shouldn't have lost my temper*, he thought. *That was ungentlemanly. And besides, they were not worth it.* He made a mental note to try to refrain from swearing at people on CBC radio in future. That might be his new year's resolution.

He checked the stove before leaving, making sure it would still be going, albeit down to embers, when he returned home later. He hadn't owned a car for over 20 years, so the walk into Hubbards, or hitchhiking, was never something he could accurately predict as to when he'd return home. He patted his head; yes, woollen hat on, gloves, rubber boots, two pairs of woollen socks, and an empty backpack. He grabbed his walking stick, a smooth five foot piece of alder. He was ready.

Saturday morning, nearly 10 am. *Not bad*, he thought. *A good time to set off.*

The snow was calf deep on the incline to the house. He trudged over the small bridge, crossing the frozen creek, then up the track to the road past the spacious summer cottage of his closest neighbour, an absentee German orthopaedic surgeon who lived in Munich and who might deign to spend a week or two here come August. He'd only met the owner once, over three years ago. He'd felt judged, looked down upon, so he took an instant dislike to the German. This felt uncomfortably natural to an Englishman.

Eight minutes later he was standing beside the old 329. It was a snow-blown highway, but the plow had been through earlier. His gaze settled on a red-tailed hawk circling above the frozen lake across the road. The sky was cloudless, egg-shell blue. A brisk day.

It was eerily quiet. *At least ten below*, he thought.

With no sign of cars coming or going, he began to walk. The village of Hubbards was about 12 miles away. On a good day he'd get picked up anywhere between where he lived and Birchy Head. The locals knew him, so he always stood a good chance of a lift. But there had been days, many days in fact, when he had not gotten a ride in at all and had walked the full route, which took him about four and a half hours at a steady pace. For a man in his early sixties it was tough going, but he never complained, except when it rained. Nobody likes getting soaked to the skin.

John Burton was a fit man, if slightly undernourished. He liked walking, always had. As he moved quickly through the light snow on the edge of the road, he recalled how he and his younger brother Edward, or Teddy, spent many happy hours during the summer holidays walking this peninsula together. All legs, shorts and long socks in those days. Teenagers.

He had always loved this part of the world. It brought back fond thoughts of his mother and father again, too. He'd often thought of them as brave souls. After all, they had packed up their old life in England, risked everything, and came to this country with nothing more than hope and dreams, the search for a better life. But mostly it had been for their children.

Was it a better life? John wondered now. He smiled as he headed down the road toward Southwest Cove, because he knew that 30 years ago he would not have even thought of contemplating that question. And if asked, his answer would have been an unequivocal "yes". But those days were the heady 1970s, when he was living a wonderful life, the high life, in Toronto, Montreal and Halifax. Young, free, an excellent career, the proud owner of a racing green MGB, Harris tweed jacket, Peterson pipe, a healthy head of hair and a steady girlfriend. It had all been going along so swimmingly back then.

A Chevy pick-up truck going in the opposite direction honked at him; John waved, but didn't recognize the driver. The Anglican church was coming into view. This was usually a good place to get picked up at. The road to Southwest Cove cut across in front of the church, and there was quite the community scattered throughout that cove.

He stopped on the corner for a small breather, waiting. The

roads were quiet. Not a soul about. Too cold to stand still for too long. Ah well, onward. Then he heard the hum of tires on snow getting closer.

He looked over his shoulder. Larry Dauphinee's beige Datsun came flying around the corner but didn't stop. Larry never did.

Just as well, he thought. That man had always driven like his backside was on fire. John tried to remember how many cars Larry had rolled over the years. He gave up counting after six.

He was near the bottom of the hill in Northwest Cove, and across the road was the old Gates house where the Brixtons rented. Their maroon Volvo wasn't in the driveway. Trevor was probably out grocery shopping with the boys. He half-wished Diana would see him passing and invite him in for a cup of coffee. But she didn't, and he walked on.

He felt the coins in his pockets jingling, metal sacks hitting his thighs; all those quarters, pennies, nickels and dimes. He remembered a time when all the coin he had was put into those yellow plastic seeing-eye-dogs stationed in supermarkets and at drug stores. But not any more. Then he wondered why he didn't see those plastic dogs as much as he used to. Perhaps they were too easy to pinch.

Since falling on hard times he'd learned the value of keeping his coins. He'd also learned what shame can feel like at a busy checkout when a miscalculation means that one of those cans or packets goes back to the grocery shelf. It's hard to look people in the eye when one is poor.

As he walked up what was known locally as "Millionaire's Hill", overlooking picturesque Northwest Cove, he stared out on Horse Island, his thoughts returning to those happy summers spent around here. He thought about his family at the cottage. His mother in the garden, knitting or reading, sometimes tinkering on the upright piano; his father on the porch playing his beloved Mozart on the violin, eyes closed in deep concentration. Older sister Elizabeth, gabbing on the telephone to one of her many admirers, always laughing louder than was necessary.

And Teddy, head buried in some science magazine, or half-asleep in the hammock. Dear Teddy...

Many was the time he'd wished to see his brother again; to catch up, share a cool beer, go fishing, or just walking, walking for miles along the coast together, swapping jokes, talking about books, girls... life. Like they used to. Sometimes he felt Teddy's presence walking beside him, and sometimes he would talk as if his brother was still around.

Teddy had not grown old. He never thought he could be jealous of that, but his arthritic knees did make him wonder.

Carl Miller picked John up near Birchy Head, taking him the rest of the way into Hubbards. Carl was a building contractor. For most of the ride he was on his cell phone, sorting out a problem on one of his work sites. The air became blue as he yelled down the line at perceived incompetence. John just smiled and enjoyed the scenery. He'd seen and heard Carl like this many times before now, but he remained amazed how quickly Carl could lose the plot. He had nothing on Carl's short fuse. Not many did.

At the supermarket he bought his meagre provisions: cans of soup, baked beans, tea, white sandwich bread reduced for sale, and some Quebec brie that had a half-price pink sticker on it because it was one day away from its best before date. At the checkout he dug the change out of his pockets, painstakingly counting it out for the rotund gum-chewing cashier, who was kind and helped him count, thanking him for the change without any hint of sarcasm.

John looked at what was left in his hand: $3.92. That would easily buy him a couple of coffees at Bonnie's diner.

Carl was waiting in the parking lot, his task at the hardware store completed. Another string of lights for the tree. He hoped he'd not messed up. Lucy was very particular.

As John left the supermarket, he called out, "John, give you a ride home?"

"Thanks, Carl, appreciate that very much. You leaving now?"

"Yup."

"Oh, alright if I go to the post office first?"

Carl smiled, nodded. "I'll wait."

At the post office, John cleared his box of junk mail and picked up one lonely Christmas card with English stamps on it. It was from his sister, Elizabeth. He put it in his backpack.

Before he went back to the parking lot he quickly popped into the Hubbards library. Connie Wilkinson, the librarian, handed him a week's worth of library copies of *The Chronicle-Herald,* which she always put aside on the off-chance he'd drop by. He thanked her and apologized for having to leave in a hurry. On any other Saturday, they would have had a bit of a chat, but not today. She smiled and wished him a merry Christmas. He wished her the same.

The ride home was uneventful and mostly silent, apart from the radio. Carl liked to listen to the local station, and on Saturdays they played hits from the 1960s and 70s. When David Bowie and Bing Crosby's version of 'The Little Drummer Boy' came on, Carl turned up the volume a notch or two. His fingers tapped a beat on the steering wheel as he ruppa-pum-pummed along with Bing. John joined in, too, each man trying to 'out-Bing' the other. They laughed.

When the song finished Carl turned the radio off. "Best version of that song. Just love it...Hey, what're you doin' for Christmas?"

Carl, as was his manner, always sounded gruff even when he was asking a run-of-the-mill question. He caught John a little off guard.

"Oh, nothing planned, Carl. Not yet."

Carl nodded. "You'd be more than welcome to come an' have Christmas dinner with Lucy an' me, if you like. It'll be just us this year. Kids aren't comin' home until new year."

"Thank you. That's very kind."

Carl's cell phone rang just as he slowed and pulled off the road near the snow-filled track that led to John's hidden house. "Let us know soon if you're coming. Lucy likes to plan things, you know what women are like...Hello, Carl speaking!"

John watched as Carl turned his truck around, cell phone still stuck to his ear. He wound down the window and called, "Merry Christmas!"

"Merry Christmas, Carl. Thanks!"

The truck fish-tailed slightly as Carl stepped on the gas and took off along the snowy highway.

It was just past 1 pm. John walked home with a spring in his step. It had been a fortuitous day.

He could see thin wisps of smoke rising into the clear blue sky as he approached the little bridge. The old house always looked beautiful blanketed in snow; all its imperfections, its unsightliness, were masked. Winter helped him forget the chores he could not afford to accomplish.

He looked forward to opening a can of pea soup and having something hot inside his belly. Connie had given him a lot of newspapers to get through, and there would be enough natural light to read by until about 5 pm. Then he would re-heat what was left of the soup, toast some bread, and have that for his dinner. Later, he would light some candles, listen to the radio.

After the nine o'clock news, it would be time for bed, bringing to a close a most satisfactory day.

He sat down at the kitchen table with a cup of tea, and with a knife he opened the envelope from England. The card was heavy and expensive. It depicted a tasteful watercolour of a country church covered in snow, with 19th century people walking toward it.

How like Elizabeth, he thought, and smiled.

As he opened the card, a small black-and-white photograph slipped out onto the table with an English twenty-pound banknote for company. It was the photograph that held him.

Inside the card, after the usual Christmas salutations and below the hugs and kisses, she had written, "I found this in an old school book of mine the other day. I thought you might like it."

He took the photograph and placed it near the window beside the radio. Teddy stared back at him, grinning like the Cheshire cat; and beside Teddy, there he was, also grinning. Two young men dressed in short-sleeved shirts, shorts, walking sticks and backpacks. The world at their feet. A photograph that their sister had snapped in the summer of 1958, right outside this house when it, too, was beautiful and strong.

He moved to the wood stove, sat down and warmed his hands.

Daniel Lillford

He stared into the flames.

It was nearly 3 pm when he got up and walked heavily up the stairs to his cold bedroom. He closed the door and lay on the bed, staring at the ceiling.

He could see his breath.

The window pane rattled.

17: The longship

Amy knelt beside him looking into a face she barely recognized. There was nothing there, not Grampy, just the pallid funeral mask of an old man gone from this world. She could have been staring at a wax-work dummy. At times the old man looked positively macabre, the way the dawn light moved across his face in the gently rocking boat.

She held his cold, gnarled hand and stared at a patchy fog bank rolling in with the sun. The smell of gasoline mingled with the freshness of the sea and the chill of the morning air.

Her thoughts were a confused mixture of uncertainty and determination. There was an emptiness in her gut, a loneliness she couldn't shake off, and she wondered what kind of shit she was going to get into after this morning's work was done.

Waves slapped the prow and the wind rose, pushing the small boat against the skiff. She watched her grandfather's face jostle with the movement of the sea. He looked odd out here, dressed as he was, crumpled into his Sunday best dark blue suit. She should have thought about his clothing, what he usually wore every day, what he was comfortable in, but that had escaped their plans and it didn't really matter now. No, not now.

~

Henry Arthur Norman, known as 'Buster' to his friends and just plain Grampy to his 14 grand-children, was 84 years old and still had a handshake like an iron clamp. Be that as it may, Dr. Samakovski had told him that he had less than a year to live. He got that diagnosis a few months ago, a week before Christmas.

Henry had thanked the doctor for his seasonal gift, but the irony was lost on the pulmonary specialist, originally from Zagreb.

~

The old boat-building shed back of Norman's wharf had always been a sanctuary for all the Norman fishermen. Generations of them had hidden away there to drink, play cards, and generally escape marital bliss. In Henry's grandfather's time the shed had stored barrels of Prohibition booze, the days when rum-running made far more money for the family than lobster or mackerel fishing ever could.

Nowadays it wasn't used much other than for storage, a place for old fishing junk. Nobody stopped there any more, and that was why it would be perfect for Buster's secret.

~

A few days before March break, Amy Jewers got a message via the school secretary, Ms Himmelman, that her grandfather would be picking her up after school. Slightly surprised, Amy wondered why. When she was a little girl he'd often pick her up from the elementary school in Hubbards, then take her for an ice cream at the local diner, but those days were long past.

She was in grade 11 now, and she'd not seen Grampy Norman since Christmas dinner. That was the last big family get together before the second COVID lockdown came along and put everyone's life on hold. She thought she was probably going to get a talking to, because no doubt her mom had told him about the run-in she'd had with the local RCMP after she got her license suspended for driving without a seat belt in an uninsured vehicle.

Awesome, she thought. *Just what I need.*

~

Simon Corkum turned the palm sander off and pushed the goggles off his eyes so they protruded from his forehead like the eyes of some dust-blown, skinny mantis. He slapped the gunwales with a rag, then stood back to admire his handiwork.

It was the most expensive coffin he would ever make, but that was what Buster wanted and that was what he was getting. Simon was building a small Viking longship, sitting a little over eighteen feet from stem to stern. It was going to be a slender vessel, flexible and light, lapstrake construction, overlapping planks that were riveted together.

He'd studied a Norwegian karve's design from old drawings. The Norsemen used karves along the inshore as cargo vessels, and as war ships. They were known for their speed.

He ran his hands over the gunwales, moving slowly up toward the headless prow, where Buster wanted to make the dragon's head himself. Simon took out a cigarette from a Players pack and lit up. He poured himself a black coffee from his battered tartan thermos, leaned back against the bench and stared into the dusty, smoky world he had inhabited for the last six weeks.

It was raining steadily. The only natural light in the shed came from a double-sash window overlooking the workbench. The panes were loose, dirty, and rattled, and three were cracked. There was a small glimpse of the cove between overgrown alders and wild rose bushes that brushed up on the window panes whenever the wind picked up.

Glancing from corner to corner, he saw history from generations of men who had made their precarious living from the sea etched into everything. Tuna harpoons with copper spearheads from the days of the schooners and mastmen. Homemade barrels filled with glass buoys, colours ranging from clear to amber, and many shades of green, in varying sizes. There were ancient swordfish blades and the bleached jaws of a bull shark taking up part of a wall. Cork floats, wooden ship pulleys on fraying ropes in rafters bulging, spilling over with cotton netting from a gentler era, when fishing products didn't harm the environment, when cotton nets and hemp ropes that were lost at sea disintegrated in a matter of months, not hundreds of years like the petroleum-based nylon

Daniel Lillford

rubbish used today.

Simon shook his head as he thought about so-called progress, wondering why man continued to move forward into a hell of his own making.

The remnants of a wood stove lay, partially-dismantled, opposite the workbench. There had been some mornings when he had wished that stove still worked. A sooty chimney rose up through the rafters. It creaked and moaned when the wind blew hard.

On the north side of the shed was a wall of woodworking tools, all a good boat-builder could ever ask for. He marvelled at the range of planes and spoke shaves, draw-knives, chisels and saws. All the tools were in very good condition. Years of respect hung on that wall as well as craftsmanship built to last.

Most of the spoke shaves were from England, some nearly 150 years old, and original *Stanley* tools from Connecticut. They had bought the best to last a man's lifetime. There was nothing cheap or disposable here, just pure class. He smiled at the collection and thought about making the old man an offer for the lot.

When Buster Norman had called him over to meet at the old boat shed back in late January, he had pushed a small leather case in front of him without any ceremony and said, "Youse are the best damn boat-builder on the South Shore. Now, listen, because this is what I want youse to do, an' I knows youse have other contracts, but this one goes to the top of your list. It's urgent. Take this as incentive. Tax free."

Simon smiled as he recalled the old man's face staring at him, the iron grip of his hand on his arm; then the shock of opening the case and seeing $40,000 in cash.

~

The green Lincoln Town Car was waiting outside the high school on Duke Street in Chester. Amy smiled when she saw it. Grampy was at the wheel; she'd recognize that nose anywhere.

She got in and closed the passenger door. The old man looked at her and smirked, then started the car.

"Got any tattoos yet?"

Amy looked at him and scowled. "Nope." She rolled her eyes. He always asked her that question every time he saw her.

He winked, then put the car in gear and moved off. "Good. Keep it like that if youse want to be kept in the will."

She smiled, shook her head. *He's lost some weight*, she thought. *His shirt collar looks too big for his neck.*

He parked the Lincoln at Bayswater beach and stared at the ocean. Amy could tell he had something on his mind because from Chester to Bayswater he'd said almost nothing apart from boring comments about the weather, and Grampy never talked about the weather unless it was to come-from-aways.

"Wanted youse to know, and I don't want youse talkin' to your grandmother neither, less she knows the better...The doc says I've got maybes a year to go, no more. Told me that jest before Christmas, the thoughtless sonofabitch."

Amy wasn't quite sure what to say. She felt tears well up but she wasn't going to cry.

"Now, your grandmother'll want to have me buried at St. boring Barnabas with all the trimmings, she bein' the high Anglican she is an' I'm supposed to be. Well, to hell with that nonsense. It's not what I want. It's not what I've ever wanted."

"Grampy, why're you telling me all this?"

"Got a job I want youse to do. Can't trust the others. Figured youse'd understand, help an old man fulfill his dying wish; allow him to go out the way he wants to go out."

She stared at him and half-smiled because she instinctively knew her grandfather wanted her to break, or bend, the law to suit his purpose.

"It's against the law, if that's what you're wondering."

Amy almost laughed, turning away, as if he'd just read her thoughts. "Why not ask one of the boys? Why me?"

"Told youse, can't trust 'em. They'd tell their mothers, sure as bears shit in the woods, an' then she'd find out and scuttle my plans. Youse can keep secrets, they can't. That's why."

He started to cough, a rasping rattling sound that seemed to shake his whole throat. He turned away from her as he reached for a handkerchief and coughed into it. She didn't see the drops of blood he brought up.

"So, I get in trouble with grandma, and that's okay, is it?"

Henry glanced at his granddaughter, then returned his gaze to the sea. His breathing seemed heavier. "It'll be worth your while."

Amy scoffed and her face reddened. "If it's money you think I worship, I'm no whore. Get someone else."

She tried to open the door but felt his hand holding her arm. His voice was pleading. "Please, Amy, don't...There'll be a letter left with my lawyers, I'll explain everything. My reasons, your involvement. You'll be helping me out, nothin' to do with anyone else. It's my death. I decide. I don't want to go into the earth...Can youse understand that, girl? The sea's where I belong."

She stared at him and, for the first time in all the years she'd known him, she saw a chink in his stoic demeanour, a vulnerability she'd never seen before now. If she didn't know him any better, she'd almost think that he was scared. "Will they put me in jail?"

"Nope. But you'll sure piss off the Undertakers' Union."

She looked at him and shook her head. "Mind telling me what exactly you want me to do?"

"Ever heard of a Viking funeral?"

~

His left hand shook a little but his right hand was still stable as he chiselled gently around the mane of the dragon's head. Simon watched him, admiring his deftness and artistry with the small chisel.

"See all that whittling over the years has come in handy, eh?"

Henry grunted and kept at his task. "When I worked the longliners youse had plenty'a time to kill out there. Man needs a hobby or a mistress. One or the other. One woman was enough for me, so I took up carving. Used to make all me Christmas presents out at sea. Never happier than when I was on open water."

Simon lit up a cigarette. He could tell that Henry did not approve by the glance he gave him, but he said nothing.

The old man looked at the rough-hewn dragon-head in the vice. He grunted and appeared pleased with his progress. "Bit'a sandpaper, almost there now."

"Seems a pity to burn it."

Henry stared at Simon and grunted, looked at the longship and shuffled off, taking in the craftsmanship as he walked all around it. His eyes watered and he stifled a cough. Simon noticed he reached for a handkerchief and brought it up to his mouth, but suppressed the cough.

Henry wheezed a bit, then ran his hand over the stern. "The auld ones came from there. Norway. Place called Lillefjord. Where my seed came from. My name, Norman, means Norse-man. I've lived my entire life on the sea, just like my father, and his father, and his father before he. One generation after another. The sea is my home. She's in my blood and it's where I belong. Don't need no bit'a grass and a cross marking my last stand in yard full'a bible thumpers an' landlubbers. That's not me. Never was."

Simon nodded as he looked toward the oak mast he was going to be working on next. "Think the girl can manage it? Lot to ask, Buster..."

"Youse jest help her get me aboard when the time comes, Amy'll do the rest. Girl's smart. Gotta brain that thinks in the moment. Rare enough these days."

Simon stared at the craggy, tanned face of the old man. When he looked into his eyes it was as if he was looking into the sea itself in all its grey-green wisdom, its brooding fury, gentleness and stubbornness, all rolled into one unfathomable depth of humanity.

~

It was a warm afternoon in May. Amy was walking out of school heading for the bus when she saw a white Jeep Wrangler parked out front. Her grandmother, Betty Norman, was standing beside it.

She was a small, lithe woman dressed in a turquoise pants suit, a blue rinse in her perfectly coiffed hair, looking totally out of place in the throng of laughing, yelling, boisterous, raggedy high school students bursting out of their institution.

Amy didn't second guess her intuition. She knew that her grandmother's famous radar was up and running, and that was why she was here.

She had never been close to her grandmother. Their relationship was formal, respectfully restrained and distant. Amy knew that Betty did not like the fact that her youngest granddaughter rarely attended church any more, Christmas and Easter aside, but as she wasn't the only teenage grandchild who didn't go, she couldn't give Amy a sermon about that particular failing. Still, Amy wasn't about to tell Betty that she was an atheist.

There had always been a certain coolness between them, one that Amy had never really understood. She remembered a Christmas when she was no older than eight, playing pond hockey with her cousins, where she body checked her much older cousin, Tyler, Betty's favourite grandchild, and he broke his nose upon hitting the ice. Her grandmother flew into quite the storm over that. If Grampy hadn't intervened, Amy always felt that her grandmother might have hit her.

Over the years she'd stayed away from the old woman as much as possible, preferring the company of her grandfather. So a reputation came about, and the family considered Amy Jewers a tomboy, or Grampy's girl. She was the only granddaughter who hung around the lobster boats, helping her Grampy, her father and her numerous uncles. She liked being on the boats, out at sea, and she was no slouch when it came to hard work.

Betty Norman, matriarch of the large South Shore fishing family, was a deceptively-frail-looking woman who dressed sensibly and was always aware of the image she wished to project within her community. She had dark, alert, piercing eyes that never seemed to blink. She could smile and scowl simultaneously, and she had a dreadful habit of putting people on edge with her perfunctory manner, a manner that often came across as prying. She was perfectly acidic and without qualms when she thought it apt to put someone down in mixed company. She was a woman who had never put up with a fool in her life and dealt with all foolish behaviour accordingly.

She was also graceful and witty, and could, when required, turn on the charm like a tap. She was the long-standing St. Barnabas church treasurer, served on various committees, and was considered the best bridge player on the South Shore. Betty Norman was equally loved and feared, had been for years, and she was perfectly comfortable with that. If she were an animal, Betty would surely belong to the reptile family.

They sat in the Jeep as Betty fiddled with the air conditioner. "Silly thing's on the blink again. Bear with me...Little bird tells me you've been seeing your Grampy a fair bit these past few months."

Amy shrugged. "Bit, I guess. Never really thought about it."

"Care to tell me what he's been getting up to? I know he's up to something. Been very secretive of late."

She was always direct if nothing else. Amy stared at her grandmother. "How would I know what Grampy's up to?"

Betty chuckled as her face tightened. She indicated, then slowly pulled the car out from the curb. "You know you're his favourite. Always have been, ever since you punched those boys in grade four, wasn't it?"

Amy smirked, nodded. That was a day etched in her memory. Both her parents called into the principal's office because their daughter had dared to beat up two little shitweasels who'd made the mistake of picking on her in the playground and calling her names.

"He likes fighters, always has. He's also dying...Oh, yes, I know. He thinks I don't, but dear old Henry was never much of one for keeping secrets. Besides, people talk. The right people do, at least."

She stared at Amy, as she turned the Jeep out of Chester and toward Bayswater. "You did know he was dying?"

Amy bit her lip and nodded. "Yup."

"I guessed, correctly, that he'd tell you."

Amy stared out of the window as the Jeep moved down the old 329. "I like spending time with him. Helping out. That's all."

Betty smiled, then patted Amy's leg. "You're a good girl, in your own way. Thank you for your kindness. I know Henry appreciates it, too."

Amy kept her eyes on her grandmother's bejewelled, frail hand still patting her knee, which was exposed through her ripped jeans. She stared at the perfectly-painted, peach-coloured nail varnish.

"I don't want to think about Henry going, but unfortunately life doesn't stop for my thoughts. Plans still have to be made, set in motion. Duty…what's expected…that sort of thing."

"Grampy's funeral, you mean?"

Betty nodded. "St. Barnabas will be overflowing that day. I doubt they'll have enough room. Everyone will come. It will be a beautiful service. I've already thought about the hymns…You should come to church more often. You should… Yes, it will be a good send-off for Henry. One that Lunenburg County will remember for many, many years."

Amy looked at the ocean flashing by and said nothing.

~

Most mornings Henry stopped by the boat shed to see how things were going. Over the summer, now well into August, each day had brought Simon closer to the reality of the old man's impending death. He had watched Buster's weight loss with some alarm: he had never seen anybody lose so much weight in such a short amount of time. Buster's clothes now seemed to droop off his frame, his face was gaunt and pale, cheekbones stretched the skin, his eyes were sunken, he stooped, and his breathing was much more audible.

He said little. It was as if talking hurt him, or it was just too much of an effort, too much energy. The coughing was worse, sometimes quite violent. When Simon had first seen the blood-stained handkerchief he'd almost called for an ambulance there and then.

Henry shuffled about the workshop, his steps reminiscent of a toddler trying to walk. He stood by the longship and smiled at the dragon's head, now sanded, stained and varnished on its curved prow. Simon knew that that was the closest look of pride he'd ever seen in the man. He knew he was satisfied.

The whole boat was shellacked, shining brightly in what sunlight hit it through the dirty window panes. The canvas sail was neatly furled, and below the mast there was a small platform where Henry's body would lie. Simon caulked and explained what he was finishing up, but Henry didn't seem to be there that morning. He was elsewhere.

It was the last time Simon Corkum saw Henry Norman alive.

~

September arrived, and with it an early fall. The poplars were divesting themselves of their yellow foliage, the chestnuts were dropping their brick-coloured leaves and the maples and oaks were turning golden, red and orange. A tapestry of colour filled the forests, the gutters, roadsides and driveways.

Betty Norman held her husband's hand for the last time at the ICU in Halifax. The life support machine had flatlined and Henry was gone.

They transported his body to the funeral home in Hubbards. The visitation was three days later.

~

Amy watched a tide of masked people come and go in an orderly fashion, COVID restrictions, social distancing, still in effect, as they paid their last respects to Henry 'Buster' Norman, who lay in state like venerated royalty. Hundreds signed the visitors book. Many were moved to tears, and many a story was told that she would never remember, but had smiled at, nodded at, laughed at, as if grateful for such anecdotes, such knowledge.

If she was thankful for anything, it was that her cousins and siblings had to do their fair share of the work, which left her time to scour the defences of the funeral home, keeping a close eye on Martin Hennigar, the funeral director.

Betty was like a gracious host receiving guests at an embassy ball. She wore a black pantsuit, and one string of pearls; her hair had been recently coiffured with a purple wash, and her nails were plainly varnished. She greeted all the guests by name, refraining from hugs and handshakes.

Her favourite grandson, Tyler, all six foot six of him, square jaw jutting, stood by her side like a mafia bodyguard. She held onto his arm for support and comfort throughout the visitation.

Getting the key to the back door of the funeral home turned out to be not so hard after all. She'd observed Mr. Hennigar, who was in charge, shadowed him well, and found what she hoped she was looking for. During a break in the proceedings, exploring an office she took to be Hennigar's, she found some keys hanging on a hook. The back door that led out onto the car park, that was the key she needed.

Finding the right one, she extracted it from the key ring, pocketed it, then put the keys back where she'd found them. She'd looked for an alarm system but couldn't see one. Which made sense to her, because who in their right mind would want to break into a funeral parlour?

When Simon Corkum got her attention around 8 pm, she just said, "Back of the building around 3:30. Be careful."

He admired her pluck, her confidence, but worried about being an accessory to stealing a corpse.

~

Amy didn't really sleep, just lay on her bed listening to music on her iPhone. As the Arctic Monkeys and The Cure ran through her brain, she kept seeing distorted images of her grandfather from when she was very young right up to the visitation. A cavalcade of people she knew locally, if not by name then by face, kept walking in and out of frame, all expressing how sorry they were.

When the clock turned over at 2:30 am, she got up and pulled on a black hoodie. Borrowing her brother's mountain bike, she started riding toward Hubbards. As the cool morning air hit her face she went through a mental list of all the things she needed to do.

First on her list was making sure the skiff was in place at Murphy's wharf.

~

Simon's rusty Chevy Cheyenne rumbled through the sleepy village of Hubbards in the early morning darkness. Nothing stirred apart from a few raccoons and some deer he startled with the high beam.

He parked out back of the funeral home and waited, but not for long. The back door opened and he could see Amy standing in silhouette. She motioned for him to join her.

In the blue shadows of night they stood opposite each other with Henry Norman's casket between them. Simon was nervous, he wanted a cigarette. Amy showed nothing but quiet resolve.

They nodded, then pushed the casket on the gurney down a carpeted hallway toward the back. Simon reversed his truck as close to the back door as was possible.

Then, and not without some difficulty plus a few muffled choice words, they lifted the oak casket and slid it along the truck bed. Amy went inside, returned the key to its rightful place, then shut the door on the way out and heard the lock click. She put her brother's bike in the truck alongside the casket, then joined Simon, who was smoking when she jumped into the passenger seat.

"They'll kill you. They killed my Grampy."

"So will not wearing a seat belt. Put it on, please."

She smirked and did as she was told as Simon put the truck in gear, tossed the cigarette out of the window, and slowly moved out of the parking lot with the strangest cargo he would ever carry.

~

The tide was due to go out at 5:13 am, so they had just over an hour to accomplish everything. Simon opened the old boat shed's wooden double-doors, putting them back on their hinges to reveal the unique outline of the unusual boat.

He pulled the trailer the longship was resting on into the early morning light, and Amy caught her breath as the dragon's head prow slid closer toward her. Simon wheeled out the little longship and hitched it to the back of his truck.

In his head all he could hear was Buster's instructions. *Take her to Murphy's wharf, the old corduroy slip. Launch her from there. Safest place.*

Simon looked at Amy, who was gently running her hand over the boat, the dragon's head.

"It's beautiful. It's... so fine..."

"Thanks. Buster made the figurehead...Well, best get him settled."

Amy nodded, but it took her a long minute before she could stop staring at the longship and get in the truck.

The drive to Murphy's wharf took five minutes, but Simon cut the lights, not wanting to attract any undue attention as he drove into the sleepy little fishing cove.

They opened the casket and stared at Henry Norman.

"You take his legs," he said.

Henry's body was not heavy. He was a shell.

Placing him on the small platform beneath the mast had its difficulties, made all the more awkward by the manhandling and manoeuvring of someone they both loved and cared for. Simon made sure the body was lying flat, the feet facing the prow, then from underneath the platform he pulled out twined bundles of straw and sticks of wood, exposing them from all sides around the body.

He looked at Amy, who had gone very quiet. "Something wrong?"

Amy reached over to her grandfather and undid his tie. "He hated ties. Called 'em 'halters for men'."

She threw the tie into the bundles of straw and sticks.

The sound of someone running and getting closer stopped them in their tracks. In the quiet they could hear the steady thump thump of sneakers hitting the road.

"Shit. That'll be Vern, forgot about him. Runs every morning, Sou'west cove to Birchy Head and back."

"What'll we do?"

Amy shrugged. "Carry on, guess."

Vernon Lutwick, a small, hairy man in his mid-forties, came around the corner and never gave them a second look. He was in his running zone.

"Mornin', Vern," she said.

Never breaking stride or looking at them, he said, "Mornin'."

They watched the jogger heading up the incline known as Millionaires' Hill. Simon shook his head, then turned to unhitch the trailer.

With Amy's help, Simon gently rolled the longship down the corduroy slipway. She watched it bobbing gently as Simon tied it to the shore.

"Did you bring gasoline?" she asked, almost in a panic. He nodded and pointed to the back of his truck.

She breathed easier, then moved toward the wharf, where she untied a small motorized skiff. She stepped into it as she pushed it to rest beside the longship.

Simon passed her the gas can as she tied on a tow rope. "You be careful. With all that fresh varnish she'll go up quickly."

"I will. What time is it?"

Simon looked at his watch. "Just on five now. Plenty of time."

She nodded. "Best get going all the same."

"Right. Good luck. Got matches?"

Amy patted a pocket, smiled. "Thanks, Simon…for everything. Helping him, I mean."

Simon grinned. He watched the girl start the skiff's motor. A few pulls and it was running. She raised a hand as she slowly headed out from the wharf, the longship trailing in her wake.

He walked on to the wharf, sat on a lobster crate, and lit up a cigarette, watching the boat he had created for a funeral moving beautifully behind the skiff.

In fifteen minutes Amy had passed Horse Island and was into St. Margaret's Bay. She cut her engine and drifted with the tide just past Owl's Head. Bobbing on a placid sea with barely a breeze, she wasn't sure if this was what her grandfather had in mind.

She looked at his corpse and half-smiled, and still found it hard to believe how quickly the end had come. It blew her mind that one day she was talking to him, then the next morning he was being rushed to the hospital.

The last thing he had said to her as the paramedics put him in the ambulance, in barely a whisper, was, "I always wanted to go there...Norway..."

She had held his rough hand in hers and cried like a baby.

Simon watched the dawn break upon the ocean. Golden threads of light danced across the water in ripples like so many unanswered questions to life's riddles and circumstances. He saw smoke slowly rising out at sea.

Amy waited for the flames to engulf Henry Norman's body, then she lowered the canvas sail and tied it off to the tiller. Simon had been right: the shellac caught quickly. Fire was ringing the vessel at speed.

Deftly moving back into the skiff, she let the tow rope go. A breeze came in from the west and the longship's sail luffed to half-strength, filling out like a set of lungs taking in new life.

It darted forward with the tide into the new day, burning and sailing through the fog bank. She marvelled at its speed, its grace on the water, its magnificent keel, as it faced into the eye of the rising sun.

"Goodbye Grampy," she whispered, "I hope you find Norway."

She was smiling through her tears as fire overcame the longship, attacking the mast and canvas as it continued to sail on its journey into the afterlife.

Ghost Breezes

Daniel Lillford

18: The truck

The sight of Lily Coolen's large beige and yellowing underwear hanging on the washing line always made Jeff Jewers smirk. He looked at the sagging material and thought of cow udders. Clothing left out in the rain is a sad sight.

He lit a cigarette and smarted. His jaw was bruised and his left eye half-closed. Luke Boutilier had a helluva wicked right hook. He thought about the fight they'd had on the government wharf the night before. Another senseless exercise in manhood, one he'd lost if anyone was keeping score, and sure as shit someone would have been.

He moved from the lounge room window that looked out on the picturesque cove and into the kitchen. His ribs hurt, and he wondered if some might be cracked.

His uncle Augie was sitting at the table, thumbing through *The Chronicle-Herald*. He glanced up at his nephew, but said nothing.

"Mornin'."

"Yup. It is. Just."

Jeff pretended not to hear, went to the fridge and took out a carton of milk. He looked in the cupboard above the sink and pulled down a box of Cheerios, then a bowl from the drying rack.

"Youse look like shit."

"Yup. Feel like it, too."

"Seldon wanted to know where youse were this mornin'."

"Tell him?"

"Nope. Nothin' to do with me." Augie flipped a page in the newspaper and continued scanning.

Jeff looked at his uncle and sighed. "Thanks for nothin'."

"Your foolishness, son. Youse fight your own battles on your own time, not on the man's who pays yer wages."

His uncle got up from the table, went to the coffee pot and poured himself out a brew. "Lucky for youse the engine played up some, spittin' oil out everywhere. Got towed back by Bo Langille. So nobody worked today, otherwise I'd say you'd be lookin' for work elsewhere tomorrow. All the same, if you've got any brains, you'll see Seldon and apologize. He's old school, like me."

He patted the boy on the shoulder then turned to leave.

"Asshole went back on his word."

"So says you."

"It's the fuckin' truth, Augie!"

"Don't cuss!" Augie clipped Jeff across the top of his head with a playful tap.

"Sorry, but just thinkin' 'bout it boils me up some. Youse know he promised me. Sonofabitch went an' sold it to some fella down in Tantallon. Tells anyone who'll listen that we never had no deal, that I'm makin' shit up. Said that in front of 'em all. What the hell was I supposed to do?"

Augie smirked, drank his coffee. "You're just lucky his brothers weren't there yesterday. Think on that for a minute or two. An' call Seldon!"

Jeff stared at his half-eaten breakfast. For a second he wanted to throw the bowl of cereal against the wall, but that would only prove what his uncle already thought of him, that he was a juvenile hothead with too much lip.

He wandered down to the government wharf around lunchtime. Luke Boutilier's brand new black Chevy Silverado was parked beside his Cape Islander, the *Get 'er Done*. Luke and his brother, Mark, were loading lobster traps onto their boat.

Luke and Jeff shared a glance, and Jeff saw that Luke had a nasty cut above his right eye and bruising on his cheek. Mark stared hard at Jeff and looked as if he was going to spring at him, but his brother said something under his breath, and they carried on with their task, ignoring him.

Jeff walked upstairs into the wharf office, where he found Seldon seated behind an ancient wooden desk, doing paperwork.

The old man looked up as Jeff came in. He grunted. "Augie send youse over?"

Jeff sighed. "He told youse? I don't believe it."

Seldon chuckled. "Nope. Just guessed."

"Right. I'm, I'm sorry 'bout this mornin', Mr. Morash. Won't happen again."

Seldon looked at him. His dark blue eyes did not blink, searching. "My mother, god rest her, used to say that the man who uses his fists has just run out of ideas. Heard youse called Luke Boutilier a liar to his face, in front of the Langille boys, Dan Murphy, Dougie Hennigar, too. That right?"

Jeff nodded.

"Then youse should know, if yer brains weren't stuck up yer arse, that youse left him no choice. Luke, like his brothers, only has so many ideas allotted to him. He ain't no professor."

"He went back on his word, Mr. Morash. An' then he lied about it to me in front of everyone there. Made it sound like I was a goddamn lying fool."

Seldon stared hard at Jeff, then he shook his head, disappointed. "Thought youse had more sense, youse bein' a Jewers. Your dad were alive, he'd take youse out back of the wood shed and knock some sense into yer."

Jeff shrugged. "Lost my temper, that's all."

"All over a truck?"

"Yup. A truck."

"Worth it, son?"

Jeff glanced at the craggy-faced old man, with his shock of woollen white hair. He shrugged, glanced at his boots, looked away, sheepish. "Don't feel like it today, knows that."

Seldon pulled open a drawer and took out a half empty bottle of rum and a tumbler. He uncorked it and poured himself a snifter. "Your godmother's Iona McRae, right?"

"Yup. Relative of mom's. Why?"

Seldon got up from behind the desk, rubbed his hair vigorously, then looked out of the window toward the brightly painted boats tied up at the wharf. "More ways of skinnin' a cat than getting' beat up for nothin'. Oughta talk to your godmother, maybe. Wouldn't be surprised if she's already expectin' youse to call."

"Oh, youse think the local witch's gonna help? I don't think so. Besides, she scares the b'jeezus outta me, always has. Eyes like a friggin' cat." He shuddered.

Seldon chuckled. "Still scares a few around here, I shouldn't wonder. Some got good reason to be scared of Iona McRae. Knows more than most 'bout where the bodies are buried. But she's a very old lady now, be near 'nough to eighty...Might give her the time of day all the same. Ain't gonna kill yer."

"Why?"

"Reckon youse were cheated, don't yer?"

"Damn right I was."

"Then go see the old lady."

The graveyard beside St. Cuthbert's church was strewn with autumn leaves. Philip Cottesloe, the sexton, was fighting a losing battle with the wind as he tried to rake leaves into a pile. An old lady watched him from the picket fence and chortled to herself as he tried to get an orange plastic bag to stay open whilst he lifted a pile of leaves toward it, all to no avail.

This farce continued on like a Buster Keaton movie scene for some minutes. The sexton threw the rake on the ground and yelled something unintelligible as he wrestled with the bag, which almost took off into the forest like a damaged kite.

Iona McRae hadn't had a good laugh like that since going to see some live theatre in Halifax, at the Neptune, 30-odd years ago. She tried to remember the name of the show as she trudged home, her thin arms full with bags of groceries, but it didn't come to her.

She thought about her old friend, Selma Dorey. It had been two years since she had passed away. Last night she had dreamed of Selma again, when they were both young women in the 1950s, and they were at Bayswater beach, swimming together. Her friend, in the dream, kept swimming into open water, but Iona couldn't follow her out. Her legs had become very heavy and she couldn't keep up. She had to return to the shore. When she looked over her shoulder she saw that Selma had turned into a beautiful dolphin

Daniel Lillford

and was happily spinning out of the ocean and diving beneath the waves, frolicking in a blissful world, if not a heavenly world. She had wanted to play with her, but it was as if she was shackled to the beach, a mere spectator looking in on a snow dome, albeit without the snow.

She had awoken with a strange sort of start in the morning; 6:25 am, the bedside clock told her, and her heart was beating fast. She got out of bed, found her well worn slippers, and shuffled off into the kitchen to put the kettle on.

Framed portraits covered the lavatory walls. Most depicted an era forgotten to time, images of a black and white world now lost. Many of the pictures showed youth, happiness, Selma and herself. An occasional magazine picture of Elvis Presley broke the feminine monopoly. Places and people, automobiles, a school, a church wedding, a home. A loved one.

She sat on the throne and pondered her erratic heart rate, wondering if she should go into Hubbards and see the doctor.

$40,000 for one bluefin tuna. Sold to Tokyo before it was even shot. That's how you know if the season's been worthwhile. A big, shiny, new truck, fully paid off, in the driveway. But the Missus still gets all his work clothes from the thrift stores.

There were six bluefin caught in the Boutilier trap come August. Most weighed in between 280 and 350 pounds. The one sold to Tokyo was over 450.

That's a lot of high-grade sushi.

Jeff Jewers, like many of the other fishermen in the cove, was jealous of the Boutiliers' success that summer. None of the other tuna ranchers had done so well; most would barely break even. It had been a bad season for them.

The big fish were not as abundant as they had been in previous years. Which was odd, because they had been told that the bluefin stocks had been rebounding since 2011, so it was not an endangered species as such; but this year the big fish seemed to bypass St. Margaret's Bay, and nobody knew why the migration pattern had changed.

All the fishermen knew was how much money they were losing.

Luke's old Chevy Cheyenne truck had served him well over the last few years, but, as he said to Jeff Jewers one night at the Shore Club, "If we does well with the tuna this summer, I'm getting' me a new truck, no fuckin' bones 'bout it."

'I'll buy the Chev off youse if yer do," Jeff said.

Luke swigged his beer, looked at Jeff, and said, "Five grand, she's yours, bud. But only if the season works out."

They had shaken hands on it and laughed. There were no witnesses to this agreement that Friday night at the pub in early June.

"Well, bless my soul..."

Iona hadn't seen her one and only godchild for almost a decade, at least not since he still trick or treated. Those were the days when children still plucked up enough courage to come to her house, before all that malicious witch gossip started up.

But there he was, ambling up the dirt driveway. *Same walk as his father*, she noted...*But what on earth had happened to his face?*

When Iona opened the door, Jeff thought at first that she wasn't going to let him in. She observed him without taking the chain from the latch. "What happened to your face?"

He shuffled, looked around nervously, shrugged. "Aw, youse know. Stuff."

She unlatched the door. "Best come in if youse are."

He caught her eyes as he walked over the threshold; they were like bright buttons, more like an otter than a cat. Her face was as yellowed as lamb's velum, a face like a road map to a city he did not know and felt very uncertain of.

Her thin spindly hand was under his chin before he knew it. She looked into his face, into his one uncovered eye, and smiled. "Wondered when I might see youse again."

Augie Coolen smoked a cigarette as he sharpened his fish gutting knife on a whetstone. The rhythmic sliding of the blade on stone took him away for a moment or two. He thought about Millie Trask, and wondered what had become of her. They were young, and for one long summer back in '85, they thought they were in love. The old East River drive-in. He smirked at his thoughts.

Intermittent chatter from the radio in the wheelhouse made

sure he wasn't lulled to sleep on the job; still, he didn't notice Luke Boutilier was there until a shadow crossed his light and he squinted to see who it was standing above him on the wharf.

Augie noticed that Luke hadn't had the fight with his nephew, a much younger man, go all his own way. That was quite the cut above Boutilier's right eye. He stopped sharpening the blade.

"Don't want no further trouble with your nephew, Augie. Best youse let him know that."

"Oh." He took the cigarette out of his mouth and stubbed it out under a rubber boot.

"Boy's gotta big mouth. Don't want no more lies bein' spread about."

Augie looked at the knife, satisfied it was as sharp as it should be. "Lies, was it? Fightin' 'bout lies was youse?"

He half-chuckled to himself. He put the knife in its holster, then looked at Luke. "One thing I knows 'bout my nephew, Luke, I'd trust his version of the truth over yours any day of the week."

Luke stared hard, then a disbelieving grin spread across his face and he looked skyward. "Yeah, well, I appreciate blood bein' thicker than water, family an' all, but youse tell him just the same. He carries on the way he does, spreadin' shit 'bout, I won't go so easy on him next time."

"That right?" Augie leaned over the gunwale and spat into the water. "Tell youse what, Luke, youse fight Jeff fair, you'll get no trouble from me. But if Mark or John gets involved, I'll personally see to it that you'll be joining my nephew in the hospital. An' that's a promise, my son."

Luke turned on his heel and walked off back down the wharf to where the *Get 'er Done* was moored.

"So it's revenge youse seek, is it?"

Jeff looked at Iona. He fiddled with the cup of tea she'd made him, too polite to say he didn't like tea. She didn't drink coffee.

He shrugged, looked at his boots. "Man broke his word. Lied 'bout it, like there weren't no shame in it. Did that in front of the fellas, people I've got to live with, work beside, in this cove. Why we fought. Stupid, maybes. Can see how some might think that, over a promise an' all, but... Seldon, he was the one figured I should come talk, talk to youse."

"Seldon, that old coot! Why'd he send youse here for?"

Jeff couldn't meet her gaze. He looked away. "Said youse might help, that's all."

"The old witch might help, youse mean?"

She laughed to herself, sipped her tea, then she seemed to drift away momentarily. She looked at Jeff, but it was as if she was looking through him. It made him nervous. "Your mother had the gift. It's a McRae thing. Follows the female line. Some men, too, the rare ones. Did youse know that?"

"Gift?"

"She always saw things, knowing things in advance."

He shrugged, uncomfortable. He remembered all right, but chose to forget. There were times, as a child, when he'd predict things, and he couldn't explain why. He'd see events in dreams, local, international, and he'd tell his father and mother about them, but it scared him. Many were the nights he'd stay up as late as he could so he wouldn't dream, usually falling asleep at school the following day, then getting into trouble with the teachers. His grades suffered. He hated those early teen years, hated those dreams.

He was fifteen when his father died; after that the dreams rarely came. Now he slept soundly, and for the most part remembered nothing. Which suited him fine.

"How's your mom likin' living in Calgary?"

"Okay, I guess. Says she misses the cove, but... Comin' home for Christmas."

"Youse need to find a dead skunk."

"What?" He wasn't sure if he'd heard right.

"Yup. Next skunk youse see, road kill, youse pick it up..."

He looked at Iona as if she was off her bean.

"Then you'll go to the graveyard back of St. Cuthbert's, where you was baptized, not that you're interested, an' at midnight, before the lobster season starts, that's two Sundays away, youse bury that skunk in the nor-east corner, near the fence."

"What good's that goin' to do?!"

She gave him a cold look. "An' youse say these words once you've buried it." She closed her eyes and recited:

> No thief will take what's mine an' kin. No words of falsehood stand in time. Over land, nor air, nor waters still. Mine enemy will fall upon his lies an' homespun sins will bring demise.

Jeff looked at her, slightly dumbfounded. "Are, are youse really a, a witch?"

"Don't talk nonsense, boy. If I was, d'youse think I'd be livin' in this old shack?"

He smiled. "What will happen if I do this? I don't want nothin' awful happening to him, just teach him a lesson, is all."

She looked away, smiled secretly. "What is meant to happen will happen. Trouble will come in three, for thee or he...But if youse have no patience, this will wither on the vine an' nothin' will change."

"Can youse write, write it down?"

She grinned, exposing her tiny yellowed teeth. She got up and took a sheet of paper from the notebook near the wall phone. She was writing as she spoke, not looking at him.

"That necklace you got your mother for Christmas, best get rid of it."

"How'd, how'd youse know about—?"

"I know, it's enough. Woman it belonged to was not a good person. Bad luck written all over it. So youse take it back to that antique fella's store in Hubbards. Get yer money back."

She handed him the piece of paper. "An' make sure youse burn this after youse say it."

He looked at her writing, small and neat, old fashioned cursive. He folded it and put it in his shirt pocket.

The tea was cold. He placed the almost full cup on the table.

For a second or two he thought he heard voices singing, faraway voices. He gave his ear a thump, shook his head, thinking he must be hearing things. He figured he was far too young for tinnitus.

Iona looked at him and grinned. "If youse look outside, an' be quick 'bout it, youse might see my little friends." She indicated the kitchen window that looked out onto the edge of the forest.

He rose slowly and walked to the window, glancing back at Iona, who urged him to look outside, which he did. At first he wasn't sure what he was looking for.

"Jeezus!"

Iona laughed.

Jeff came upon a dead skunk on the old highway near Blandford. He made sure that the coast was clear coming and going before he got out of his rust-ridden Honda Civic and approached the dead animal.

Grabbing the creature by the tail whilst holding his nose, he put it in a *Sobey's* grocery bag, then threw the bag in the trunk whilst trying not to gag on the stench, a stench that permeated his whole vehicle in a matter of seconds. The acrid smell would stay there for many weeks to come.

He was glad to get home and put the animal out back of the woodshed.

As lobster season edged ever closer, preparations at the government wharf were becoming feverish, with all the fishermen engaged in tasks and chores. Boats were being fixed up, cleaned, repainted; engines made ready; lobster traps piled up on decks, looking like mini–skyscrapers. The wharf never seemed to shut down as that final week of November bore down in its own steady rhythm of life.

Jeff went about his job with Seldon and his crew and he kept his nose clean. He avoided drinking at the Shore Club and, most importantly, he steered clear of Luke Boutilier and his brothers.

This did not go by unnoticed. Augie, for one, was impressed with his nephew's sudden venture into maturity. He liked the fact that Jeff was now getting out of bed in the morning without him having to raise him. And often the lad was up even before he was.

Seldon was more circumspect, and he watched Jeff like a hawk. Still, he quietly hoped that the boy had inherited his father's trait, and was exercising patience like he'd never exercised it before.

This pleased the old man, but it also bugged him.

One day, in the office, Seldon asked Jeff, straight out, "So, did youse go see Iona?"

Jeff didn't want to answer, but he couldn't lie. He nodded. "Yup. As youse suggested."

"She help youse out some?"

"Might say that, guess."

Seldon didn't say anything for a minute. He continued to look at paperwork in front of him. "Youse didn't ask her for nothin'...bad?"

The question floored Jeff. "I don't know what youse mean, Mr. Morash."

The craggy faced old man looked up, but he was not smiling. He looked almost scared. "Don't take me for no fool, son, an' don't take what Iona McRae says as foolish neither."

There was a lull. The ticking of the big old railway clock on the wall, the occasional shout from men on the wharf filled an otherwise silent exchange between them.

"She just said that trouble would come in three, for him or me. Like some kind of riddle. That's all she said."

Seldon nodded, rubbed his hair in that nervous way of his, got up from the desk and looked out of the window, watching the men working on the wharf.

"To be honest, I'm not sure I know what the conversation I had with her was all about. Strangest afternoon I've ever had, tell youse that for nothin'."

Seldon grunted. "Youse should know that Luke's been mouthin' off 'bout youse down at the Shore Club, 'bout the fight youse had. Says next time he's goin' to put yer in the hospital."

"I've been stayin' away from trouble, Mr. Morash. I've said nothin' to him since the fight. Stayed clear of him an' his brothers. God's truth."

"I knows that, boy. An' it's probably jest the beer talkin'. But best youse stay on yer guard, is all."

Jeff Jewers found out the prophetic meaning of Seldon's warning later that day. He was driving in his old car, happily cruising along the Bayswater foreshore at dusk, when a large black truck came up behind him quite suddenly, high beams on, blinding him with the reflection in his rear view mirror. It was right behind him, butt-hugging, moving left to right in an agitated manner.

The truck overtook and squeezed in front just as an oncoming vehicle rounded the bend up ahead near All Saints' church. The truck put on its brakes, forcing Jeff to do likewise—which sent him into a slight fishtail as his all season tires didn't quite grip the road well enough, and he skidded on to the shoulder.

He recognized the truck as it sped off into the dusky light in a burst of high octane and rubber, leaving him shaken and angered. The sound of the dragging muffler from his old Civic told him that the rust had finally won that battle.

He pulled further over on the shoulder, thumped the steering wheel and cussed. He cussed a number of times. Luke Boutilier's ears would have been burning.

It was the Sunday night before the start of the lobster season and the small cove seemed unnaturally quiet. The wharf was ominously silent. Boats lay filled to the gunwales with lobster traps, gently moving, scraping on tire buoys against each other, against the wharf. Some were three abreast, bobbing together on a gunmetal sea. Weather was cold, but not unusual for November. Flurries were expected later that evening.

Jeff paced around his bedroom, smoking a cigarette. He took Iona's spell and read it again. He must have read it over ten times in the last hour or so.

In a fit of frustration, he screwed the piece of paper up and threw it against the wall, where it promptly bounced back at him, hitting him on the forehead with some sting to it. This surprised him so much that he started to laugh.

He smoothed the paper out again and spread it on the small desk near the window. For a minute he thought he had heard Iona chuckling, and he turned quickly, looking around his room.

It was a ten-cent moon. The graveyard beside St. Cuthbert's was still, but a ghost breeze played momentarily with what few leaves weren't sodden or already decaying underfoot, sending them into and through the picket fence.

Daniel Lillford

Jeff had decided to walk through the cove via the forest that backed onto it. His car might have attracted undue attention, given its present condition. He'd wrapped the decomposing skunk up in a number of plastic bags, but its stench infiltrated everything. It was not a pleasant walk.

As he came upon the track that led up to Iona's cottage, he slowed down, listening carefully, moving cat-like. The wind rustled the few remaining leaves on oak and ash trees, but otherwise it was peaceful. He smelled wood smoke.

The thought of what he had seen, or what he thought he had seen, out back of Iona's cottage, quickened his feet. He remembered his mother once talked about little people in the forest, but he had never believed all that nonsense about fairy roads and mounds. Now he wasn't so certain.

He checked his watch again; 11:40 pm.

As he dug the hole with some urgency, he felt as if the whole world was watching him. After he buried the skunk, covering the grave with twigs and leaves, he hastily took out the spell, then looked at his watch again. Four minutes to go. He breathed heavily, looked around.

"What the fuck am I doin'?"

But whatever doubts he might have had, and he had many, he continued. At exactly midnight he recited what Iona had instructed him to do. He said it, and as he said it he concentrated hard, picturing Luke Boutilier's face and nothing else. Then he took out his cigarette lighter and set fire to the piece of paper, letting it burn on the small mound of dirt.

Somewhere close by a twig snapped. Jeff gripped the shovel and peered into the darkness. He heard a snuffling sound, like a small pig grunting in the undergrowth, and then a porcupine came into view.

Jeff breathed easier. He quickened his pace and left the cemetery as fast as he could walk.

Out of the shadows Iona stepped into partial moonlight. She watched Jeff disappear back along the trail into the forest, then she moved toward where the skunk was buried, walking around the grave, almost trance-like. She started singing quietly to herself as she moved, but it was not in English verse. It sounded much older. Gaelic perhaps. If Jeff had waited and stayed in the secrecy of the forest, he might have seen that Iona wasn't alone.

It started to snow.

Dawn had not even broken, but the wharf was a beehive of activity. Engines kicked into gear, ropes were unfastened from bollards, and heavily laden Cape Islanders moved away from the wharf...all but one.

The *Get 'er Done* was getting nothing done. The engine sounded like crap.

Luke was not a happy camper. He was yelling at Mark and John, looking for blame, for incompetence. Tempers were flaring between the brothers.

Fishermen from the other boats laughed and shouted out cheeky jibes, shared cynical homespun wisdom, openly revelling in the Boutiliers' misfortune. Schadenfreude was never so pointed as it was today, the start of the lobster season.

As Seldon's boat moved away from the wharf, Augie at the wheel, Jeff couldn't help but smile. They passed the *Get 'er Done* and Luke did not appreciate seeing Jeff Jewers grinning from ear to ear. He called him an insulting name referencing his lineage.

Jeff just shook his head, started laughing, then he gave Luke the one finger salute and turned away.

The boats streamed out of the cove at speed, heading toward Horse Island and into the open water of St. Margaret's Bay and the lucrative lobster grounds.

It was to be the first of a few problems that Luke Boutilier would face that week. The diesel engine on the *Get 'er Done* had to be repaired or replaced. A piston had broken and scored the cylinder walls, and she was toast. This inconvenience set him back days. When the other fishermen had returned home after laying their traps, the *Get 'er Done* bobbed forlornly against the wharf, loaded with traps and nowhere to go.

If Luke had been feeling sorry for himself, which he had, he'd probably have been better served not drinking to excess in the local tavern that night, then trying to drive home. The Mounties had set up a checkpoint at the Hubbards turn-off to the 103, and Luke sailed right into it.

They impounded his brand-new truck and left it in the car park, and took Luke to the Chester detachment's lockup, where he was charged with drink-driving.

He called his brother John, to come pick up his truck and take it home. But, unfortunately for him, a thief had got to the truck first. It was gone when John arrived. It's still missing.

A few days later Jeff and Augie were getting ready to go and check their traps when Seldon came out of the office and strode up to where the boat was moored. "Youse heard the latest?"

Augie and Jeff looked at each other.

"What's goin' on?" Augie said.

"Luke Boutilier's in Bridgewater hospital."

Jeff felt sick in his stomach. Seldon watched him with a solemn gaze.

"Jeezus, serious? What happened to him?" Augie asked.

Seldon paused, scratched his head and looked most concerned. "Gettin' his appendix out."

The three of them shared looks, then one by one they started to laugh.

"Lordy... That poor fucker's cursed!"

Seldon and Jeff looked at Augie, shared a grin, but did not comment.

Iona was picking up a few logs from the woodpile in her old barn when she heard Jeff calling out her name.

"In here, boy! The barn!"

He stood in the doorway, saw what she was doing, and moved quickly to help. "Youse shouldn't be doin' that, not at your age."

"Why not? I'm not an invalid yet."

He took the wood from her spindly arms, shaking his head. It was then he noticed an old red truck at the back of the barn, covered in dust and planks of wood, half-tarped, its tires as flat as pancakes, and cobwebs all over the place.

"What's that?"

"My old truck, what's it look like?"

Jeff smiled, put the wood down and walked over toward it.

"1949 Dodge Fargo," she said with a hint of pride.

He ran his fingers over the truck's distinctive, long-nosed hood like he was patting a fine horse. The red paint was faded, almost pink in patches, there was some rust, and she sure needed some work done to her, but Jeff was falling in love. A '49 Dodge Fargo. He couldn't believe it.

Iona smiled as she watched him.

"Youse...youse want to sell her, Iona?"

"Might."

"How much?"

"Oh, well that depends..."

He looked at the frail old lady with eyes like an otter, wondering what mischief she was up to now.

"Could be I need someone to help me out round the house few times a week. Someone I can rely on to get me supplies when I needs 'em. Someone to bring the wood in. Fix things that I can't fix no more...Someone to play cards with once in a while. I like crib."

Jeff nodded. He looked back at the truck. "Reckon I owe youse. The truck, she was yours?"

Iona, for a brief second or two, saw herself and Selma Dorey standing beside the Dodge when it was shiny and new and they were young, both dressed in their bathing costumes.

"Once upon a time, yup. Still is. Just old now, like me. Forgotten." She laughed, then started to cough.

"Time youse had a cuppa tea, Iona."

She smiled at him. "Youse hate tea, knows that."

He took a small package from his shirt pocket. "Why I brought me own coffee, yer old witch."

She laughed. He picked up an armful of wood and walked past her toward the house. She glanced back at the truck, shook her head, then moved out of the barn.

They sat beside the wood stove with their respective beverages. Jeff felt at peace, the most peaceful he'd felt in years. "I still get them dreams, like when I was a kid. But not so often now. Hardly at all these last few years."

Iona nodded. "Scared you a lot, back then, remember that. Your father was so worried 'bout youse."

"Was he?"

"Oh, yup. He worried all right. Truth is he worried 'bout everythin'. Stan was like that. Good man. His nature I guess. What killed him in the end, I reckon. Worry. Lesson in there for youse, boy."

Jeff nodded, sipped his coffee. "Had a dream 'bout him not long after he'd gone. Saw him standin' on a rickety old wharf, god knows where it was, an' he was fishin' for mackerel. The sun was bouncin' off the water an' he, he was smilin', that big wide goofy grin of his, an' the fish were literally jumpin' off his line, an' he was puttin' them in this bucket. He was so happy. When I tried to reach out to him, I couldn't move. Like me feet were anchors, youse know. I couldn't touch him even though I tried. It was like he was behind glass or somethin'."

Iona closed her eyes and smiled. "Yup. He say anythin' to you, in that dream?"

Jeff nodded. "Said, 'I love youse, son.' An' then he turned back to the sea, carried on fishin'. An' slowly, slowly, it was like I was disappearing down the end of a telescope. He was gettin' further and further away from me until I couldn't see him no more. Haven't dreamed of dad since. Miss him, knows that."

"Nothin' unusual in missin' those that youse love. Reckon they walk right along beside us until it's our time to go. Sometimes youse'll feel a shadow, a presence, might even be scent, a smell, like perfume or aftershave, in a room. Somethin' that was theirs... See, love never dies, jest bodies, like worn out coats. But love never dies."

Iona got up from her chair and put the empty tea cup on the sink. She looked out of the window, catching her reflection in the glass. Standing beside her was a young Selma.

"What was the point in me buryin' a skunk at midnight?"

Iona looked at him, a wide grin filled her lined parchment-like face. "Oh, that was just to see if youse had it in youse. Nothin' more."

"I knew it. I friggin' knew it!" He looked at her and shook his head. Then he started to laugh.

She glanced out of the window into the encroaching darkness, smiled, and whispered something inaudible.

Daniel Lillford

19: The promise

The German carving knife protruding from his ribs went in easily enough. Louise considered it for a time, and then reached for the handle. It came out much the same. She wiped the blood off the blade with a tea towel.

Charles' eyes were open with a look of total surprise.

Yes, it would have been a surprise, Louise thought.

Putting the knife in the sink she proceeded to wash the dishes. The small radio blurted out the news on the hour, but she turned it off after a few minutes of depressing bombing reports from Palestine and awful COVID stories coming out of India.

"Nothing but war and death," she said as she stepped over her husband's body and put some dishes in the cupboard.

Dusk had descended before Louise knew where the day had gone. When she thought about what she had done all day, she vaguely remembered watching a few episodes of Seinfeld. Everything else was a blur. Lunch? Did she even have lunch?

Photographs of her four children stared at their mother from the mantelpiece. They were all living in other provinces. She was glad, especially today.

Louise reversed the lawn tractor up to the back door, turned the engine off and dismounted. In the kitchen she tied some rope around Charles' ankles, then opened the door and hitched him to the John Deere.

It seemed strange to be going over the lawn with her husband's body bouncing along behind her. He'd loved his lawn tractor and had always enjoyed cutting the grass to within an inch of its life. Somehow it seemed almost sacrilegious.

But what the hell, she thought. Fuck him.

Daniel Lillford

The light was fading fast when she got to the fire pit and dragged his body over the narrow brick area into the charcoal circle. She untied the rope, then took a breather. Their farm looked small, a lonely silhouette on a hill, and yet they were one of three farms on this stretch of road. Still, the lack of lighting from the neighbours' dwellings, one not more than half a mile from their house, made her feel quite alone.

She felt for the matches in her jacket, then grabbed a gas can from the lawn tractor. For the next twenty minutes she arranged kindling and logs around Charles Veinot's body, then liberally poured gasoline everywhere. As she struck the match she took one final look at him, then sent him into oblivion.

Louise watched the flames leap into the night and thought about a song by David Bowie, and without meaning to be disrespectful to the departed, she started singing quietly to herself about putting out fires with gasoline.

As the fire burned down, she remembered happier times with a man she had loved very much; walking along a snow-white beach hand in hand, newly betrothed, sexually satisfied, together and in love. She thought she'd found her true love, her soulmate, her best friend.

That was in 1985. And now, at sixty years of age, she was alone again. For a moment she wondered where life would go from here.

She cried silently.

It was nearly midnight when she returned to the house. A terrible burgundy stain blotted the kitchen tiles. She stared at it for some time, remembering when she'd first found lipstick traces on his clothing.

At the time she hadn't thought much of it, but as his Thursday night Legion meetings seemed to drag on more than usual these past few months, she began to have niggling doubts, and then suspicion started to weave its sticky web. About a month later she decided to follow her husband into town. She gave him a twenty minute start.

Parking in a side street with a good view of the Legion entrance, she sat in her old Jeep and waited for hours until the lights in the building went out one by one and all the patrons had shuffled off on home. Still there was no sign of him. Part of her wanted to go home, drive away, but her instinct told her to stay put.

When he finally emerged, he was not alone; that tubby girl from the drugstore, all tits and ass like a collapsed muffin, and way younger than his own daughter, was hanging off of his arm. Louise watched them kiss and fondle each other in the shadows as betrayal clasped her heart and squeezed.

Charles Veinot was a handsome man in a faded-glory kind of way. Over the years she'd noticed quite a few women taken in by his tanned looks, his flashing smile, his laugh. So it came as a bit of a letdown to see him with Ms Tubby. Louise had expected…well, she didn't really know what she had expected. She only knew she felt sick, empty.

All those years ago, on their honeymoon, he'd laughed when she'd promised him that she would kill him if he ever broke their vows and slept with another woman. He'd made light of her. Of course she wasn't serious, she was just kidding around….

But it wasn't a joke; not then, and not now.

~

As he switched the coffee pot on, Charles barely heard his wife's accusations. It was early morning, he was foggy, though still thinking about his mistress on the carpet in the president's office at the Legion the night before.

When the knife entered his body to the hilt, he turned and stared at Louise, but there were no words. His breath had vanished…

There was only the silence of shock and the sight of the small hand that let go of the weapon as he slid to the kitchen floor, where the last thing he saw were the yellow kitchen tiles.

Daniel Lillford

20: Davey and the dolphin

It was an uncommonly quiet morning. None of the usual banter, no ribbing, joking, just the occasional blurting radio chatter aboard the *Lucy May*.

"Over there, see!?"

Seldon Morash and Augie Coolen stared hard at the mackerel trap-net suspended by cork and coloured buoys in the grey seas off Horse Island, but saw nothing unusual as dawn broke across the waves in streaks of gold.

"There! In the trap!" Young Davey Trask pointed, jabbing his finger into the air like a harpoon.

"Yup. I sees it," Seldon said. "Shark, maybe."

Davey shook his head. "Nope. That's a dolphin, Mr. Morash. See how the fin moves, up an' down, not straight. Gotta be a dolphin, maybe a porpoise."

Seldon looked at the boy and smiled. Davey was just like his father, Ron. He got excited, just like that. Cheeks reddened, eyes shining. Yup. Just like that.

"Eyes like a gull," Augie said, with a chuckle.

Seldon nodded as he picked up a gaff, making ready to draw up the leader rope. Augie steered the Cape Islander toward the trap, a cigarette hanging off his bottom lip, the engine of the *Lucy May* chugging them closer toward the circle of buoys that enclosed a quarter acre of sea.

Augie revved the boat, then cut its engines, and the *Lucy May* bobbed gently in the wash as it sidled up alongside the trap. Styrofoam buoys scraped the hull, shrieking like a knife across a plate. Davey and the men tied the boat off, then Augie climbed into the green seine boat that the *Lucy May* towed behind her.

The dorsal fin of a small dolphin breached the surface, its blowhole spraying with a short gasp.

Davey was beside himself with glee. "It's a dolphin, a calf!"

"Yup...bottlenose." Augie said.

"Reckon so."

Davey, his eyes never leaving the trap, clambered into the rocking seine boat as Augie steadied her, making sure the boy's footing was sound. They watched the dolphin, a calf no bigger than a fully grown sheepdog, swimming around the enclosure, its body moving up and down in a slow rhythmic circle of the trap.

"Why can't it just jump out, Augie?"

Augie looked at the dolphin, its sleek grey body, a silver shade in a charcoal sea. He shook his head. "Not sure, boy. Maybe it doesn't know how to get out; though it chased the mackerel in sure enough, the dumb little fool."

Davey nodded. "Gee, she's beautiful, eh."

Augie smiled as he pulled on his orange rubber gloves. Seldon started up the winch, making ready to hoist the net. Davey glanced his way, a look of alarm on his face.

Seldon read it."Don't worry, Davey. We'll get that silly bugger out of there."

"He means I will," Augie said with a wink. "The old fella'll be stayin' dry,"

Davey and Augie began to purse the net into their boat as the dolphin kept on circling. Davey quietly hoped that the dolphin would just jump out, free itself from the trap.

Twenty minutes passed as the boats drew the net closer in, shrinking the dolphin's environment with every foot of netting brought out of the depths. The sun was almost above them and it was easier to see now.

The little calf was getting closer to the seine boat with ever decreasing circles, its blowhole wheezing out a funnel of fine spray.

"Don't want to get it hurt an' tangled up in the net," Davey said.

"All will be good, you'll see."

Davey couldn't see how things would be good, but he trusted Augie.

Daniel Lillford

The mackerel were visible now, pewter arrows darting this way and that, as the rising net brought them closer to the surface. The Cape Islander winch whirred and the rickety wheel feeding the leader rope clanked. It sounded like a clock in Davey's ears, each clank another 30 seconds gone by, and still the little dolphin hadn't jumped.

Then it happened in an instant. The dolphin circled within easy reach. Augie, without hesitation or warning, plunged both arms into the water like a front end loader and scooped up the calf, tossing it over the gunwales to freedom.

Davey stared at Augie with his mouth open. It happened so fast, a split second, that the boy had hardly the time to acknowledge it. The fisherman's agility amazed him. All he could do was stare, awestruck, silenced in joy.

Seldon's crag-lined granite features showed nothing. He'd seen many things over his 60 or so years as a fisherman on St. Margaret's Bay. Augie, without any fuss, had returned to his task of pursing the net.

Davey continued to follow the dolphin's dorsal fin as it moved up and down beneath the waves. Suddenly, the dolphin turned starboard in an arc and headed straight back toward the boats. Davey stared in disbelief as the little calf bounded through the waves straight toward them. "The dolphin, it's...it's comin' back!" he said.

Augie glanced up and chuckled. "Maybe he just wants some more mackerel."

"I'll give him mackerel," Seldon grunted.

The dolphin came right back to the seine boat, popping its head out of the water, staring straight at Augie, with its bright button-like eyes, showing him its fine rows of white teeth, pink mouth, making a calling sound something like "chap-chap-yack-yack," punctuated with a throaty clicking staccato vibration. It did all of this with an accompanied up and down head movement, repeated at least three times. It appeared to be smiling at Augie, an infectious wide smile of happiness. Then it disappeared below, turning away from the trap-net, the boats, and out into the bay.

Seldon and Augie stared at the departing dolphin in silence. Only the waves lapping the boat, the squeaking buoys and the cry of the gulls broke the stillness.

Davey felt his eyes moisten, the fine salt spray stung his cheeks, and his heart was full. "He came back to thank you."

Augie looked at Davey in disbelief, then back to the disappearing fin off Horse Island.

"Why he came back, Augie: to thank you. You're a lucky fella."

"Ah, go on with youse," Augie said.

Davey laughed. Augie looked embarrassed.

The men and the boy went about their fishing with blank faces, bright eyes, in private worlds.

It was about 10 am when the *Lucy May* returned to the tiny cove and tied up alongside the other Cape Islanders. The haul of mackerel was so-so, a reasonable catch.

Unusually, there was no rush to leave the boat that morning. The boy and the men kept themselves strangely occupied in minor tasks that normally wouldn't interest them in the slightest. The kinds of jobs that get done eventually, but never today. No one spoke or got in the other fella's way. They moved about like dancers in rubber boots.

Seldon's Mt. Rushmore features seemed lighter somehow, not so stern or troubled. At one point he took off his grease-stained ball cap, scratched his cropped, woolly head, laughed a little at what he was thinking, but said nothing as he cleaned the wheelhouse window with vinegar and yesterday's newspaper.

Augie lit a cigarette and stared off toward Horse Island. His eyes were glassy. He knew that the boy was right, that the dolphin had come back and spoken to him. He'd felt it and it had unnerved him. Made him feel things. Emotional things. But he didn't understand why. He'd looked into those black button eyes and seen so much warmth and kindness. It had felt like...like love. But of course, that was just ridiculous.

Davey beamed; he couldn't stop smiling. His ruddy cheeks were the hue of a Honey Crisp apple. He sat in the green seine boat for an hour or more, reliving the morning, the warm sun beating down

Daniel Lillford

on his neck and arms, his blue-green eyes on the ocean, and his heart swimming with a dolphin.

Ghost Breezes

Daniel Lillford

Author's note

People often ask where I get the ideas for my stories, which is a hard question to answer truthfully because there are so many parts involved in putting a story together. There is no definitive answer. Allow me to explain.

Sometimes I see scenes for a story in dreams, and reoccurring dreams exert their own pressure; and sometimes it is as simple as a fragmentary moment of dialogue between people, real or imagined, that I'm yet to fully understand. Very often it is simply a place, an image, like a beach, an island, a house, a forest. Places where anything can happen, places where people meet, places where something good or bad carries its own legacy into the here and now.

Environment will often dictate the action. Momentum, too, plays its part. A character travelling, the headlights of a car flashing across the windscreen at night, a boat chugging through the grey chop, a character on a journey toward some form of discovery, and perhaps a lesson in enlightenment.

And there is, of course, the ordinary everyday observations of life from which to draw. I have drunk from that well frequently when thinking about people for my characters, those who have left an impression of one kind or another. I am a grateful sponge when it comes to remembering dialogue, certain regional words, phrases, the humorous and the serious, in all its wondrous slang and coarse pithiness.

There is also the relaying of stories I heard from my elders when I was a child. A kind of layering, one might call it, like ghost stories passed down through generations of storytelling.

Last, but by no means least, I use my own personal experiences in which to infuse the fictional with the element of truth.

I see my stories filmically as I write them, often directing camera shots as I put the description down. Writing like this may have something to do with my other career as an actor. Writing and acting naturally merge.

But to be perfectly honest, I know of no other way to write. Once I start writing, I move quickly. The blinkers go on and a kind of fever takes over.

I write everything down in longhand with a pencil before going anywhere near a computer. For me there'll never be anything quite like the excitement I feel upon writing those first few lines down on paper, not knowing where this adventure might end up, or if these fledgling explorer words will even make it into the final draft.

You see, there is no map, no plan. I have no idea where this ship is sailing. I just know I have to go with my intuition, dive into the unknown, throw uncertainty and doubt into the wind, hold fast and believe.

I have always written this way. Sometimes I have the ending before I know the beginning, other times I'm stuck in the middle of a conversation that could fit in anywhere, if only I knew where anywhere was exactly. I do not like labouring over ideas for days or weeks, so I try to get that film out of my head and onto the page as fast as I possibly can.

Once it is on the page, however messy it might be, that's when the real fun begins. The jigsaw is now out of the box.

DL
August, 2022

Acknowledgements

I would like to thank the following people who have helped me shape this book through their encouragement, support, and love. Theirs were those small voices of hope that gave me breath when doubt clouded judgment and the black dog weighed me down:

Rachel Brighton; Harry, Jesse, and Rupert Lillford-Brighton; David and Sue Brighton.

Gro Ween, who simply asked to read the stories, then gave me invaluable feedback before I knew I had a collection worthy of being seen.

Jesse Lillford-Brighton, for his wonderful artwork and thoughtful conversations with his old man.

All the actors I have known and worked with, some of whose faces I used regularly when writing characters.

Jennifer Crouse at Endless Shores Books in Bridgetown.

Andrew Wetmore, my long-suffering editor, who has been a brick throughout the process, and the man who first suggested my stories might have a home at Moose House Publications.

My old friend John Dunsworth, god rest his soul, who taught me to see that there's a story behind every rock in Nova Scotia.

Ian Ball, who helped a fellow come-from-away navigate this brave new world.

And Madelaine Le Bailly, the storyteller who entranced a small boy a long, long time ago.

Daniel Lillford

About the illustrator

From a young age, **Jesse Lillford-Brighton** has interpreted and expressed nature, family, fictional characters and ideas through his whimsical drawings. In his late teens, Jesse switched to digital tools, and so deepened his artistry and the complexity of his illustrations and the stories they convey.

Jesse is the second of the author's three sons.

About the author

Daniel Lillford is a professional actor and playwright who has been working in the entertainment industry for over 42 years. He has had more than 35 productions of his plays in Canada, The United States, Australia and Scotland.

He spent his childhood in Jersey, Channel Islands; his formative years in Australia; and immigrated with his wife, Rachel, to Canada more than 25 years ago. They have three sons and live in Nova Scotia's Annapolis Valley.

When Daniel is not acting, or working on his growing collection of short stories, he can often be found walking along the Fundy coastline with his border collie. As always the lure of the sea remains a source of calm inspiration and wonder.

"The Course", included here, also appears in *Moose House Stories Volume 1*.

Lightning Source UK Ltd.
Milton Keynes UK
UKHW020046110123
415109UK00016B/1093